A'na's Gift

(Pieces to the Puzzle)

Sherri Bridges Fox

A'na's Gift (Pieces to the Puzzle)
Copyright © 2022 by Sherri Bridges Fox

ISBN: Paperback: 978-1-959151-02-9
              Ebook: 978-1-959151-03-6

The Reading Glass
BOOKS

Reading Glass Books 1 888 482 4596
www.readingglassbooks.com
orders@readingglassbooks.com

Contents

Acknowledgments

I wish to thank the angelic world and those in the unseen world for assisting me with A'na and Lucy's story. I am grateful for the insights, for the images, and for being a part of their journey, as it was my journey.

I also wish to acknowledge my gratefulness to our Source, but I especially want to express my gratitude for the gift of our lives and the beautiful world, our Earth, that we temporarily call home.

I wish to thank my husband, Terry, for supporting and encouraging me in all endeavors I pursue.

Chapter 1

Two Different Worlds

This story begins in what is now your present time as I am writing from what you consider your future. They are helping me to do so. (More about who they are on page 73.) I was a twelve- year-old girl when I first met A'na in the edge of the woods by my house. The lessons and gifts she left with me have been ever-present in my life and in my spiritual heart. My life was forever changed. It is these very same gifts that I wish to share with you.

I am now a sixty-five-year-old woman, and although she is not here on planet Earth with me, A'na is in my heart forever. She is a part of my being and I, hers. It is a bond that can never be broken. Our meeting would be one of the most wonderful, magical, unbelievable, miraculous events of anyone's lifetime, and so it was! This is especially true for a twelve-year-old girl who was so shy and timid that she could not speak up for herself.

My name is Lucy, and I am that twelve-year-old girl, that is, until I look in the mirror and realize what the illusion of time and gravity has presented before my eyes. I look back at that time in my life with a smile on my face and joy in my heart for the beautiful miracle that I was part of and continue to be.

Lucy's world is that of a small community of her family and friends. She lives in a rural area. Lucy is what you would call naive and innocent. She has no idea of some of the things that go on in the other parts of the world. Only what she may occasionally see on the television, which is seldom, and what her friends may talk about, which is not much. Her life pertains mainly to her family and the animal friends she has on the farm. She is quite intelligent, although soft-spoken and quiet. One would not know of her talents and otherworldly knowledge. Lucy does not even know of the depths of her knowledge at this point in her life. She has not awakened from her slumber on a third-dimensional planet called Earth. There are many changes taking place, and these changes have not only taken Lucy by surprise, but the world!

Hope is a four-letter word that many people have lost. Many are disillusioned by the present circumstances that is before their eyes on planet Earth. Some people have lost the idea of hope and the entire meaning of the word. Some people have lost the importance of this word. The lives of many need this little word to stay afloat, thrive, and do more than exist in a world they may no longer know. When hope is lost, so are the people. Hope gives us the feeling of expectation and desire. It gives us a feeling of trust. It gives us a feeling of belonging.

A'na has brought hope and so much more for Lucy and for others. A'na is very aware of how hope can bring light where there was very little. It is this light that Lucy feels when she is near A'na, and it is this light that Lucy will come to see, feel, and recognize in herself and in all things.

Whereas Lucy comes from a world of distrust and anger at this time on Earth, A'na comes from and lives on the planet Mentaka. She was and is such a kind and gentle person to this timid twelve-year-old girl.

She is an old soul with the wisdom of the Sages. Her life is lived with great passion and will. She knows what each and every life lesson is before it even is. She is a master of life with much wisdom and knowledge. She willingly and joyfully shared her knowledge with me. She seemed to know exactly what I needed to hear, and she knew exactly how to help me to remember. A'na knew what I needed to feel in my being as soon as I met her. We would become inseparable, at least for a while.

I am sharing my story and my gift of remembering these very special times in hopes of changing your story to one of unconditional love, open-mindedness, and a life of hope. I want to remind you that we are so much more than we think we are. A'na's gifts were not things but rather beliefs and ways of making changes in my perspectives and beliefs about life.

As a twelve-year-old, it was very easy for me to grasp and understand much of what A'na was sharing with me, although it was different than what most people were perceiving and believing at the time. I wanted to see the beautiful imagery and hear the beliefs she was sharing with me. It was easy because she was pure unconditional love. Just to be near her was like being bathed in a love so beautiful and accepting you would find your heart-melting. I found myself in the beautiful world and beliefs she presented. I wanted it to be my world! It was easy to conceptualize, imagine, and utilize all of the new ideas, perspectives, and practices I was learning from A'na. It felt right. Although I was not sure who would believe me when I told them. It was wonderful. It felt good to be a part of her world and to know there was so much more to our lives than had been portrayed. She was the perfect balm for a little girl's spiritual heart, especially in the terrible chaos and upheaval we were finding ourselves in. Her teachings would go directly to my spiritual heart. What she would share with me would change my life forever in a very profound and positive way, and maybe it will change the world you are seeing before your eyes.

This the story of our journey together here on earth, at least for a short while. These are the gifts and perspectives A'na had shared with me that I wish to share with you. I also have a very special secret I wish to share with you.

Chapter 2

Looking Back, Life as I Saw It

As I had mentioned, A'na and I met when I was twelve years old and the pandemic was all around us, in North America, Europe, Asia, India, and Africa. The pandemic had touched almost all of the world. It did not matter if you were rich or poor, old or young, the pandemic was affecting all of us and our lives as we knew it to be. There was not an area that had not been affected by this pandemic, a strain of influenza that was called Covid-19. I was just a young girl, but even I knew that our world had changed overnight. Our lives would be forever changed by this pandemic. Most people were drowning in fear, fear of all kinds. Many had lost hope. There was much turmoil and distrust of one another. Many had lost family members. Many had lost business and income, and some had lost both family members and income. Some families were hanging on by a thread and others were thriving. Our lives were being forced to change. Some of us were wearing masks, some of us not. Some of us were vaccinated and some were not. There were many arguments about the masks, who was wearing them and who wasn't. There were arguments about vaccinations. Those who had gotten the vaccinations were angry with those who had not. There was fear of the vaccine as well. It was developed very quickly to fight against the flu that was mutating quicker than we could name its new strains. There was much anger! Some people believed the pandemic was a hoax used by politicians to keep us from political freedoms. There was a great change taking place before our eyes and it didn't look good. These were dark times, it seemed. But even in those dark times of fear and death, there had been a glimmer of hope and beautiful life-changing events were taking place if one cared to notice. Many who had worked forty-plus hours a week were now home and were given a glimpse into being with their loved ones and knowing just how precious they are. Quality time was being spent with loved ones. Oh yes, there was that constant nagging about money for many. Food was scarce at the grocery stores, demand and hoarding were high and supplies were low. We would have highs and lows surrounding the pandemic as it would come at us in waves. Just as we would come out of one strain and have some freedom to move about, businesses would reopen, and another strain would appear. We would get glimmers of hope that we were escaping the pandemic. People were being thrown out of their homes because they could not pay rent, but new laws were being forged to keep people from being thrown out of their homes. The lay of the land seemed to be changing every day. Unemployment payments were at a record high and almost everyone could collect unemployment. General conditions would seem to improve, and things seemed to get better. Stores and restaurants would reopen only to realize that they could not find labor, or the pandemic was offering a new variant to be had. It seems a comfort had been found in collecting money from the government while doing nothing. Again, many shops and restaurants were forced to shut down because of this. Help could not be found for many businesses. There were not enough laborers to support reopenings for many employers. Closings were frequent.

There had been pandemics in our earth's history before Covid-19, but this strain of influenza was man-made, a biological weapon, capable of mutating into different and more powerful strains. It was a devastating blow to the whole population. Vaccines were being produced in a hurry, in record numbers. But it seems the vaccines were not keeping up with the mutations of the flu strain's ever-changing strength. We would go in and out of new Covid-19 strains, only to be placed in another deeper state of fear. A lot of money was being made by the large pharmaceutical companies; it was a fact that could not be ignored, just as large amounts of money are exchanged during wars. Could it be that the vaccines themselves were part of the weapon? Booster shots and were being made and recommended for those who had gotten the vaccinations. It seemed as each new strain was named, the public was asked to get another booster shot. A new vaccine was developed for the children. Again, there was mass confusion about giving this vaccine to our children and what the long-term consequences would be for the children. Everyone had their own opinion. It seems some of those who had gotten the vaccines were angry with those who had not. People were still getting sick after they had been vaccinated. Many vaccines were manufactured. Pills were being manufactured. Many had died from the pandemic, and more were dying. The ones dying would have other health complications that complicated matters, but this was not discussed much over the news media.

I didn't know it at the time, but I think most of us had forgotten that we were born with our own immunology to protect us from sickness. It was part of our body's own arsenal to fight against foreign intruders into our bodies. Fear does things to people and makes them act differently than they may normally act, especially fear of death as it was being shouted from every television screen, and newscast. Lines were always lengthy for people being tested to see if they had Covid. What we hadn't realized is that we had much bigger things coming in the future.

We could not run. We could only stand our ground and have faith in something much bigger than ourselves. It would be the only way to escape any of this and not panic. I knew that my grandfather had been in the war, and I would ask him if he was afraid to die. This is his answer: "If a bullet had your name on it, it was your turn to die." In other words, he was telling me that we each have a time for our passing. If we knew that time, would we act differently? Would we huddle in a corner awaiting that time? Would we go insane with worry? He said, "Live each day without worry and let God take care of the rest." In other words, "Live your life!"

As I look back, I realized that many had died from being killed by another. Anger was out of control. It seemed everyone owned at least one gun, if not more. Children were killing children with guns in fits of rage, depression, and lost hope. Many innocents were killed in the gunfire exchange. Many no longer trusted our government. We seemed to be a nation divided. We were in the middle of chaos and crisis! My world was a very scary place. We did not know what we were up against or how to get past it.

We were just coming out of two plus years with Covid when Russia decides to invade Ukraine. This war seemed to be another low point in our lives. It was a most difficult situation, and no one wanted to challenge Russia. Russia's Putin seemed to be a troubled man without conscience. It was feared that he would use chemical warfare in Ukraine if he was not getting what he wanted with all of his bombs and tanks. Why would he stop there? We watched as it seemed like our hands were tied and could not intervene to stop Vladimir Putin, the President of Russia, from what he was doing: killing innocent people, bombing everything, and everyone, homes, hospitals, apartment buildings, and cars. The news was constantly reporting and airing all of it. The Russian people were being kept in the dark and told only what he wanted them to know, but there were some who knew otherwise and protested. Several million people in Ukraine, mostly women and children, were displaced. This war only helped to fuel the anger and frustration that had been smoldering for the past two years in the United States. Most people were raw with emotions and were ready to strike out at anyone and anything. It seemed most people wanted to blame someone! He was another object to despise while we watched what he was doing to innocent people, declaring war on a nation, destroying not only families but everything that the Ukraine people had established, leaving large craters in the earth where hospitals, schools and gathering places had once stood. Bomb after bomb after bomb. Ukraine represented the most united front standing against Russia and holding their own, while all NATO and the United States were doing was placing sanctions that would only hurt Russia's pockets. We could not stop what was happening. It hurt to see it and to know it was really happening. All of the ugly just seemed to be popping up in all kinds of ways and we as a people had to deal with it as it all came flooding to the surface.

Our class had read and studied Nazi Germany. Some people do not believe this happened. Thousands of Jews were killed in Nazi Germany. Somewhere in the back of my mind, I was seeing a control that was beginning to take place and I did not like it. At some point, the adults had to keep their vaccination cards to be allowed to enter certain places. I did not like how it felt and I told myself do not think this way. It could not happen to people of our time. We could not be brainwashed in such a way as to be controlled by the government. The insurrection at the White House only added to the fear that was present everywhere I looked. They had called themselves patriots, but I could not wrap my head around it, our people hurting our people, just like they did in the civil war. They had called it a war for emancipation, but it was only in name; our people of color were still mistreated and harmed in so many ways. To me, all lives matter—black, yellow, white, and red. They all matter. Every one of us matters! Why couldn't we see that? Why repeat our history? Why couldn't we just accept one another? It hurt me and it bothered me and yet I felt powerless to do anything. I was just a young girl. Who would listen to me?

There was also another concern that was finally being recognized by the masses. It was something that I had learned about at school, climate change. We were learning and discussing how our carbon emissions were making a big change in the climate on our planet. The ice caps in Greenland and Antarctica are melting too fast. As a result, the ocean levels are changing. It is these ice caps that supply much of the clean air that we breathe and the water we drink and use daily. We were destroying our Earth. It is believed that our fate was sealed when the industrial revolution took place. The air we breathe, the Earth breathes, and all of her inhabitants breathe were changed forever. All of the chemicals, greenhouse gases, and poisons were taking their toll on our earth and our bodies. It seemed these were the things that we refused to look at and take responsibility for. Australia's Barrier Reef was dying! It hurt me to know these things. Many thousands of fish, coral, and sea environments were being destroyed. I felt powerless and all of it lay heavy on my heart. Many did not believe any of this and turned a blind eye to it. Many believed it to be just an expected change, as in our planet's history. For me, I believed the former and I was greatly saddened by what I had learned. There was a trickle-down effect that was happening and affecting our planet in a variety of disastrous ways. Many animals were about to become extinct on our planet because of our lack of responsibility and respect. I had just heard about the first country to suffer as a result of climate change, and it tore me from the frame as I imagined what these people were going through. Madagascar had been in drought for five years, even the river that ran in its midst was dried up. There was hardly any water to be found in the area, no plants other than cactus. People were starving and dying as a result. Starvation is a long and painful death, and it was taking the young, the old, and every age in between as there was no source of food, other than cactus. I knew something had to be done to help these people. I was afraid it would be too little too late.

There had to be something we could do to help ourselves and our earth from our ignorance and lack of responsibility. There are those that think someday we will have to find another planet, but why would we do that when we can't take care of the planet we are on. There had to be something that every household could do that would help to make a difference for the better in our world. Our world was looking pretty dismal. Many people were losing hope. That simple little four-letter word. The feeling of expectation and desire for certain things to happen. It would seem that without hope, a situation could become meaningless. When one loses hope the darkness takes over and the light fades from our sight. The condition of thriving ceases to be and existing takes over. Just existing, was not a life that I cared to have. I wanted my life to matter, and I wanted it to make sense. Hope is like a beautiful friend that lifts me up, that gives me the drive to carry on, to see the beauty in all things in life. We do not thrive without joy. Without hope, joy does not exist.

A'na came to Earth in the middle of all of the this change and confusion. I was certainly confused by all of it. But she also came at a time of a beautiful and great change that was taking place upon Earth, a change that many were not aware of. She came when I was just about to enter young adulthood. A'na began to share her life on planet Mentaka and her beliefs with me. As she did, I began to get a new understanding of myself and my world. I learned how to make the most of this life, to live through my heart and maneuver through the difficult times that were here, to encompass beyond what I was seeing with my eyes. I began to know that I was so much more than I thought I was. I had a purpose in this life. I didn't understand we were in the beginning stages of a shift in our consciousness until A'na made me aware with the truths she presented to me. I learned that better circumstances were coming for all who wished to be a part of our new world.

A'na presented me with pieces to the puzzle, a puzzle I wasn't even aware of and now I am providing you with the pieces of the puzzle she shared with me. We are all part of this puzzle. What one does affects the other. With A'na's guidance, I was able to see that it is our unconditional love, our care of one another, our understanding, and our compassion for one another that is the most important aspect of our lives that and being thankful and grateful for this gift, our life. I learned there is so much more to our lives and changes we can make to enhance it, but more than that, it is finding the balance of our mind, our body, and recognizing our spirit, that inner being, that will give us our ultimate life experience. I learned that instead of trying to control life, to flow with it. Our love and compassion are needed now, more than ever. This is the story of my journey with A'na. Planet Earth was just the beginning of my story. It would be the gift of remembering the secret in my heart and the miracle it held that would propel me forward in life with the teachings of a fifth-dimensional planet A'na had shared.

Chapter 3

Memories of the Past

For me here on Earth, in Statesville, North Carolina, it was a beautiful spring day, a special day for me, I might add. My family was having a small celebration for my thirteenth birthday that was coming up. My brother and sisters and their children would be at our house to celebrate. It had been a long while since I had seen them or enjoyed their presence. I was looking forward to having family come over and be with us, as our lives and most everyone's lives had been changed by the pandemic that was going around the world. We had been reduced to wearing a mask or not, getting a vaccine or not, staying home or not. The schools had been shut down. I found myself not being very happy. I missed my friends at school, and I missed being with my family. I wished for things to be as they were before the pandemic. I longed for normality!

My childhood was a very different world from that of my parents. Their world was one of surviving from financial ruin and starvation, as taught to them by their parents. Mine had not been a childhood of want. We were not wealthy, but we did not go without. Any tech gadget, clothing, or thing anyone could want could be bought in a store or online. Fear was not part of my world, at least not until the pandemic had hit. Now, people were fearing for their lives, scared of contracting Covid-19 and its sidekicks, scared of dying. New strains of the pandemic seemed to pop up with each wave of the virus. It was in our face, constantly on the news if one cared to watch the television or look on the internet.

I knew I could find comfort in my animal friends and long walks into the woods. I could let myself forget all that was going on around me and just enjoy the moment. I had always loved being outside and was used to being by myself. I would sit and look and observe nature or just be with the animals or horses for hours at a time. This is the time I would just be lost in the moment and nothing else really mattered.

Today was special. Although it wasn't my birthday, my family thought we could celebrate when it was warm and pretty outside. We could all be together outside in the open air. My real birthday is not until Christmas Eve. I guess my family was trying to make things more normal for all of us. It was a good excuse to celebrate and come together. My mother loved family and having family get-togethers and cooking big meals for all to enjoy. It was always a good time. I just didn't know it then, but those times would be some of the best times of my life! Having all of my family close by and sharing our family bond of love.

The pandemic was hard on all of us. It was something I don't think any of us had ever given any thought or imagined happening in our lifetime. The pandemic seemed to be the one that was in control. We were no longer free to come and go as we wanted or that is what we thought because the fear had us by the hand or shall I say mind. Although my grandparents had come through some very difficult times as children, their times were that of survival. It was a fear that had been passed on to my parents in many ways. Value was placed on everything. Things were not taken for granted. We recycled, reused, and re purposed as much as we could. If their fear was the fear of survival and going without, our fear of the pandemic was that of death. We were being told to fear for our lives, to shelter at home, and to stay away from others so as not to be exposed to the virus. The other part of the scenario was to be vaccinated so as not to spread the virus. There was enough fear to go around the world several times. It is widely known that Covid-19 was a man-made virus, made in a lab in the Wuhan province of China. That is the information we were told. People were taking their frustration out on the Asian population in the United States. Many people of Asian descent were being attacked and harmed. There were many theories as to who and why. What vaccine could keep it from invading our bodies? What could we do to stop its spread?

For me, the birthday party we were about to have was better than any shot in the arm. It took my mind and my heart with the ones I love. It was going to be good for the whole family. I was very excited and ready to have some fun. I hadn't realized how much I needed people, my family around me to interact with and enjoy their company. I had always been comfortable with myself, but I needed the energy of others, even if I was shy around ones I did not know. It is a feeling I cannot describe when being around others, although I also needed my time alone to recharge. It is their energy that feeds my soul and rejuvenates me, I now realize.

For me to get to have my family and cousins nearby was a joy. It was better than the real birthday celebration. My mother and father had known what I had been missing because they too longed for the closeness of family and friends. My mother shared her love with food. Feeding her family and close friends with the dishes she had prepared put a smile upon her face. It was the giving she enjoyed. She was most happy in her kitchen preparing meals for her family. This I now know made her heart sing.

It wasn't just me or my family that was feeling this loneliness, it was the world. We were all longing to belong again. We missed the love and the closeness of having family and friends nearby or coming to visit. It is part of our makeup as a human race whether we realize it or not. Most of us love to be around others for periods of time. For me, I always had my animals and nature, but I also needed people from time to time.

For some very few people, their lives had not changed because of the pandemic. For these people, they walked to the beat of their own drum. They did not engage in social media or watch television or listen to what the news media had to say. They were not under the influence of the news media and their lives went on as normal. Fear was not a part of their lives, at least not this type of fear. For me, I didn't watch any of the news on the television and for that reason, I did not have that level of fear over subjects the media projected, although my parents watched the news every evening before dinner. I was still very aware of the situation just listening to my parents' talk. I guess not hearing the news every day was a blessing for me. I was shy and timid enough without any additional fear being placed upon me.

Chapter 4

One Day on the Other Side
of the Milky Way

For A'na, this had been an ordinary morning on her planet of Mentaka. She arose from her comfy sleeping mat to hear the birds chirping and saw the sun beginning to rise. She took a big breath of fresh air, a long stretch, and at the same time began to take notice of the first colors of the sun peeking through the darkness. All the while she was preparing to do her 45-minute meditation by the waterfall pool. She must hurry before the sun has fully risen so she can see the beautiful colors of red, orange, purple, and pink reflected in the morning sky. She knew exactly where she was going. She quickly meandered through the rose garden to the waterfall pool.

A'na lives on a planet that is mainly water. There are many waterfalls, waterfall pools, lakes, and streams as well as springs and oceans. The planet is about the same size as Earth, having eight beautiful oceans full of life. The oceans are home to many of the same creatures found in Earth's oceans: dolphins, whales, sharks, starfish, lobsters, flounders, sailfish, and many more aquatic species of fish. The water is pure and clean and has many,

17

many varied colors of blue, turquoise, and green. The sands are white and full of seashells, big seashells and tiny seashells. The beaches, as well as the planet, are pristine and beautiful. There is no trash, no electric lines in the sky or the ground, no factories, no shopping centers, no automobiles, no manufacturing, and no restaurants. It is a very natural environment. Clean air abounds. Fresh fruit grows abundantly with beautiful flowers all around. The planet and her inhabitants live a mutually respectful existence.

The waterfalls that A'na frequents offer a constant sound of moving water. The water drops from various distances of 50 to 150 feet. This is music to A'na's ears. The water is clear, clean, and fresh. An abundance of plants, fauna, and wildlife fill the planet. Most of the ferns by the water are huge, over six feet tall! Mentaka is a very beautiful and enchanted planet. The area that A'na calls home is filled with many waterfowl, fishes, and woodland creatures who also call it home. There are those creatures who may come by for a drink or just to rest by the water's edge. Many come just to visit. It is a wonderful environment, filled with people that have respect for all, the planet, the plants, the animals, and the humans. A'na has chosen the garden by the waterfall pool for her meditation because of the enormous rose garden that is planted nearby. Roses are one of A'nas' favorite flowers! She uses the essential oil she makes from the garden's roses in most of her sacred work. Rose oil holds one of the highest vibrations of all the essential oils. The roses are planted to one side of the waterfall's pool. It is mesmerizing to see all of the many colors; red, yellow, white, pink, fuchsia, purple, peach, and all shades in between. There are many, many rose bushes blooming year- round. There are also huge, beautiful arbors filled with climbing roses. As she enters the garden through one such arbor filled with yellow roses, the plants begin to nod hello as she passes by, and she nods in return. The wonderful, floral scent of the roses fills the air with perfume and Ana's heart with a feeling of love. Each rose has a very distinct scent, similar to one's personality, each having its own sweet perfume. A'na stops for a moment as she cradles the blooms of several rose bushes to inhale their sweetness. She is also sending the rose bushes her love and light. She telepathically communicates her thankfulness to the roses for providing such beauty. She can recognize each rose by the scent alone. She loves everything about the roses, their leaves, their beautiful flowers of many colors, as well as the fragrance they share. A'na loves to care for the roses as much as they love being cared for. She gently lets them know when she will be trimming their older blooms and any other limbs or leaves that need attention after her meditation. She always lets them know of her intentions so that they can prepare their energy and draw it back in certain areas as she trims. She gently leans down and caresses a nearby bush all the while thanking and praising each one as she walks by for the heavenly perfume and beautiful flowers they have so generously given for all to share. All communication is being done telepathically. A'na always hums while she is with the flowers or in the garden and often sings to them as well. The flowers always bring out the best in A'na and the feeling is mutual for the roses.

A'na makes her way to the waterfall pool in fast time, it is not very far. The waterfall pool is crystal clear by the water's edge, turning a beautiful deep aqua blue as the water gets deeper and deeper. The bottom of the pool is naturally covered with small stones that have settled into the sandy bottom. The smooth stones are a massage for the feet. A'na can see many of the fishes that call it home as they dart back and forth beneath the water. She undresses and slips her toes into the water's edge as she takes in a big breath and begins to relax more and more with each step into the water. The pool is like a natural spa in every sense of the word, soothing all of the senses. From the sounds of the water, the beautiful color, the natural fauna and the movement of water from the waterfall itself one is transported to another place. It is a very comfortable, 84 degrees, thanks to the geothermal springs. A'na loves to do her meditations in the water, as it is so naturally calming. She is surrounded by lakes, streams, and waterfalls. A'na can sense and feel each one with its different motions and noises and histories. It is a truly magical place. She is well aware of the magic that surrounds her, she takes nothing for granted in her life, but is very grateful for her home world. She is aware that it is truly heaven on Mentaka. As she walks deeper into the water, she can feel the fish gently touch her legs and feet from time to time. She walks deeper into the water and as she does so, she is aware of her body relaxing her as she is transported to another dimension. She relaxes more and more with each breath as she allows herself to slip into a very deep meditative state. She floats on the surface of the water. As she lies there, suspended on the water's surface, she focuses on her breathing and allows herself to gradually become "one with the water," gently flowing and meandering. Before she knows it, in her mind's eye she "sees" the history of the waters. She feels it in her being. She knows they are connected; they are one. She is the water. The water is her. She understands the true meaning of unity consciousness. She just floats on the water as if lifeless, her mind is a blank slate as she allows herself to be in this moment. After approximately 45 minutes she begins to come back from her meditative journey. As she opens her eyes, she sees the beautiful blue sky above her. She realizes that her eyes are filled with tears from the feelings of joy, and thankfulness she felt while in her relaxed, heart-centered, meditative state. "Her cup runneth over" as love and gratitude fill her spiritual heart. A'na lives on a very, very special planet, a sacred place for all. The water is both healing and rejuvenating. A'na is aware of the living consciousness that is within everything. She knows that the ONE has imbued all of creation with life. She knows the water; the oceans and the streams all have a consciousness. She is aware that the water is a living being. As she begins to come out of her meditation a little more, she realizes she must get ready and prepare for her work of the day as she is leaving the planet for a short investigative trip. She telepathically says goodbye to the fishes, as she comes up out of the water, she sees a Blue Heron on the opposite side of the pool. She has made a connection with this blue heron as she continues to the edge of the water where she slips her clothing back on and spends some time with the roses as she promised. She carefully trims and caresses all the bushes she can before she has to depart. After trimming and chatting with the roses for a while, she bids them ado and makes her way through the lush, green-covered hill towards her ship, promising the roses she would finish trimming the next day.

Today, it is Ana's turn to investigate a section of the borders surrounding her planet. It is a precautionary procedure that is done weekly and this week it is A'na's turn to check for anything that may be of interest or concern, any changes that might be noted. Although Mentaka is a fifth-dimensional planet, all are aware that there are civilizations living in other dimensional realities. Mentaka has been a 5th-dimensional planet for millennia, but A'na is well aware of other planets that are not.

A'na is a science teacher on the planet, as well as an historian. She has in-depth knowledge of the history of her planet and those of many other planets. She also works with the children on the planet ensuring that they have a firm foundation of this knowledge as well. She is also a mentor for the "rites of passage." Each week she teaches a different knowledge of the birthright gifts and the importance of being grateful to their Source. A'na is also responsible for teaching the children's' meditation classes, which begins at the age of two.

A'na considers her time with the children one of her favorite gifts. She gently takes these young ones into a guided meditation. It is not uncommon to see as many as twenty-five children sitting cross-legged in complete silence. Spiritual life knowledge begins at birth. Just by observing the adults, the children learn to be grateful and express their gratitude to their Source from a very early age. All life is sacred on Mentaka. The children also know that they are an extension of Source. Working with the children is something A'na had done with the assistance of her sister, Raina. She and Raina worked side by side with the children every day.

A'na makes quick time and changes from her daily attire to her pilot's clothing and readies herself for her mission. She gathers her supplies, several water jugs and picks up a few fruits and veggies for the trip. She says a quick goodbye to her family, giving each one a warm embrace. It is a day trip, and she plans to be back on Mentaka shortly after sunset. Although the Milky Way is a huge galaxy, she is checking on a small area of the Milky Way today. She will be back on Mentaka in a few short hours at best.

Mentaka is a planet in the Milky Way Galaxy. It is a fifth-dimensional planet and is located on the opposite end of the Milky Way from Earth. Although it is about the same size as Earth, it is very different from Earth in many, many ways. It has one large sun. There are two moons. The moons are cyclical twins, a most beautiful sight, especially during the full moon phase. During this time, at night, one is walking with ambient lights. The waters glisten beautifully under the two full moons' light. Mentaka is alive! Her inhabitants know she has a consciousness of her own. She is respected, loved, and honored by all who call her home. Mentaka has been a fifth-dimensional planet for millennia. Many hundreds of thousands are honored to call it home.

As A'na prepares to enter her ship, she checks the exterior for any cracks, dings, or dents and makes notes. The ship is fairly small. It measures around eight feet in width and is approximately twelve feet long. It has a smooth, shiny exterior finish, like polished silver. It is made from a special alloy that is present on the planet. It looks and feels like mirrored glass. One can see their reflection in it. It is propelled by ten large crystals which also serve as the energy source for the entire ship, including the navigation system. The entry door has her name engraved onto an emblem, and below it is the symbol for Mentaka, an infinity sign within a heart. The ship was crafted and gifted to A'na for the special service she provides for all, as she is most loved and respected on the planet. She looks at the emblem fondly as she touches the emblem and commands the door to open with her touch only. She enters her ship and gets comfortable in her ergonomically fashioned captain's chair. The chair appears to be made of a substance that looks like leather but is really a plant- based material. Inside there are two seats and many compartments. There is a 360-degree viewing window. She first checks the ten large quartz crystals that are her main power source. There are many controls, one for speed, wind force, energy input, and several navigational instruments. A'na checks the navigation coordinates for accuracy.

With everything appearing as it should, she is ready for departure. She takes flight without incident and is on her way to the halfway point as was plotted. A'na loves to fly in her ship and joyfully awaits her turn to do so. It is something she takes pride in doing as it allows her to spread her wings, to see and enjoy her planet from afar. It looks amazing from the stars. The waters appear as blue terrain from above. It looks to be a swirl of blue, white, and pink as she lifts off and enters the atmosphere above. The stars of the Milky Way are beautiful, white glowing dots against a backdrop of black. Ana sits back and takes in a big relaxing breath as she begins her trip. She is out of sight within moments.

Chapter 5

Where Am I?

A'na's trip has been uneventful as far as anything unexpected, or so she thought. Her work mission is almost complete. The controls are on autopilot. A'na is finding herself a bit sleepy and gives in to the urge to nod off. After all, she had stayed up late the night before going over the next day's lesson plans. She gets so excited when working with the children and wants the lessons to be exciting for them. A'na puts in a lot of extra effort and attention to make sure what she is explaining and teaching will pique their interest so they will want to know more, whether it is science or meditation, or spiritual exploration. She always gives two hundred percent. She decides to give in to a little recharge nap. After all, she has made this trip thousands of times and so she is comfortable in taking a little nap. She shuts her eyes, and before you know it, she is sound asleep.

When she awakens sometime later, a little startled, she opens her eyes to see that her ship has landed. All appears good until she takes her attention to the outside and she knows immediately that she is not on Menaka. She has landed on level terrain on the edge of a thickly wooded forest. She is in a grassy meadow. There is no one in sight. It is dusk. As A'na looks around she takes in the beautiful colors in the sky and notes that there is one big sun that is setting. Although she is not on Mentaka, she takes a moment to appreciate the beautiful shades of orange, red, and pink in the sky. She is constantly aware that everything in the known Universe is created by the One, our Source. "Oh, what a beautiful paintbrush our mother/father Source has!" She is not scared, but a little alarmed that she had fallen so soundly asleep, which is completely out of character for her. She reminds herself that there are never any mistakes, only opportunities. She makes some notes on her palm held computer.

A'na knows she must prepare to exit the ship. She finds herself a bit nervous to do so. She checks the read out for atmospheric conditions and is glad to see that she will not have to wear any type of breathing apparatus. The atmosphere is a bit thicker than on Mentaka. The air has many toxins and microscopic debris in it, as indicated by the atmospheric analyzer and AQM (air quality meter). It is not the healthiest oxygen, but it will not kill her instantly. She will probably fill the thickness of the air by her breathing but should adapt to it quickly. She opens the hatch and steps down onto the ground. She is surprised that the first step feels much like her home world. She sees and feels the lush green grass beneath her feet. She looks out further and takes note of the woodland flowers and the scent of the woodsy forest nearby. She sees dots of color from the many flowers in the field. She notes the white flowers on several trees at the wood's edge, dogwood trees. As she looks into the forest, she sees something out of the corner of her eye. It is a four-legged animal. It is a deer. She has deer on her planet too! There are many woodland creatures on her planet of Mentaka. She is elated to see this deer. When A'na looks up she sees many more creatures coming out to "greet" her. A'na senses they are frightened. She takes a moment to reassure them as she telepathically lets them know she will not harm them. The woodland creatures understand her communication and are a bit curious and come in closer to

A'na. They have never been addressed by humans before. They feel relieved and A'na is relieved because she is not alone. She again, telepathically connects to the creatures before her. There are several deer, raccoons, bobcats, birds, many birds, crows, foxes, rabbits, several snakes, and a mountain lion in the distance. Three bears are peeking from behind some large trees near the back edge of the forest. She sees the fairies peeking from behind some nearby bushes. As she makes her connections, she learns that they were all scared at first because most of them never have never come close to or communicated with a human. The creatures were aware that she was different from the other humans on their planet. She assured them she would not be harming any of them and was at the present moment "lost." She was not sure where she was. The creatures were elated. They let their guard down and one by one they gradually came closer to greet A'na. During her stay, she would learn much from her animal friends about their world.

A'na went to the biggest tree that she saw in the nearby forest, knowing that this tree is the oldest in the group. The old tree was a maple tree. She was a very large, and majestic tree, quite beautiful. Her limbs reached high into the sky and spread out to the north, the east, the south, and the west. The trunk appeared to be over six feet across. Yes, this tree has had her share of storms by the damage to some of her older limbs. Her roots were scattered on the ground's surface in all directions as well. She was just beginning to leaf out for the season. She appeared to have a red screen all around her with tiny green leaves just appearing and poking out. A'na could see the nature spirits all around this tree working their magic. This tree is considered a "Grandmother Tree" in A'nas' home world. The Grandmother Tree is the oldest and most respected tree in her surroundings by the other trees. She is wise and knowledgeable. She is responsible for "informing" the other trees of what is taking place, what is happening, and any pertinent information that may need to be known. Her roots are part of a large web of information, not unlike the world wide web of the internet, both receiving and sending information. A'na put her hands on the tree and stood there silently for quite some time before leaving the tree. A mutual communication was taking place. Just as she is turning to leave, the maple is sending out information about A'na. Soon all will know of her appearance and some other facts about her and her situation. As she runs away to leave, she has a concerned look on her face as she comes back to the woodland creatures.

Although the Mother tree and the woodland creatures could tell her much about the planet, she needed to explore her surroundings eventually. The woodland creatures and the Mother Tree informed A'na she was on planet Earth. The old tree referred to her as "Mother Earth." From what the woodland creatures were telling her and not telling her, as well as her studies of Earth, she already knew that it was not a fifth-dimensional planet like Mentaka. Its inhabitants were not "one" with the planet or with nature. Many were still not "Awakened." She was aware that some of her inhabitants were just beginning to awaken from their slumber, to remember their origins. Some of them were to be considered hostile and dangerous. This gave A'na pause and concern. She had read about and studied planet Earth. It is regarded as a "learning planet," or rather, the "school of hard knocks." It is considered a free-will planet. She knew it was in the beginning stages of going from a 3rd-dimensional planet to a 5th-dimensional planet, which usually means CHAOS! Although planet Earth had come and gone many times in its past, this was a time in its cycle for great change. It is called the Age of Aquarius. It is soon to be a glorious time for planet Earth, a place for those who care to join in Earth's rebirth as a fifth-dimensional planet. Before this beautiful change can happen there will be much chaos, almost like Earth is going backwards in her evolution. Darkness can seem to take over as circumstances change to expose beliefs that are no longer needed or serve any purpose.

It is darkest before the dawn. To the observer it would appear that Earth was de- evolving into complete chaos and darkness, going backwards. Many things will need to be brought to the surface to be dealt with before the next phase can take place. Many will and many have left planet Earth.

For now, since it is getting dark, A'na would go back into her ship and see if she could find out where she was exactly and how she had gotten there. She wanted to check the energy crystals but did not want to light up the meadow to do so. It would have to wait until tomorrow after sunrise. She didn't know precisely how long the night would be present. Maybe she could use the ship's log to see where she veered off course and how far she had veered, exactly. Since she was not sure of where she was exactly, she did not know what type of humanoids were present nearby, asleep or awakened, but if she was on planet Earth and her history was correct, she knew she must proceed with caution, for her own safety. She knew most were probably still "asleep" and that their consciousness had not awakened them to remember. She was not sure of the current state of affairs of this planet, given their status. Once she knew these few simple facts about the world, Earth, she landed on, she would be more informed as to what "reality" was dictating the consciousness of its inhabitants for the time being. So for now, she was taking it slow until she knew more.

It was a bit of a restless night for A'na. She had grown so comfortable on her 5th-dimensional planet of Mentaka, she knew many things before they happened. She was gifted in that way, but here she was not quite her usual self. A'na was off center a bit, whether she wanted to admit it or not. She was curious about her whereabouts and how this had even happened. These thoughts played on her mind, but she found comfort in knowing in her spiritual heart and reminding herself that there are no accidents, only lessons for the soul. She was very comfortable in her ship and had everything she needed to take care of herself and her needs for a while. She knew that her family and many others would be concerned over her whereabouts, but not worried. She knew the alarm had already sounded on her planet when she did not return as scheduled. She planned to set her beacon as soon as she had the coordinates. She would communicate telepathically through her meditation, letting her family know she was perfectly fine and would return when her ship was repaired.

The early morning sunrise was here before she knew it. She exited the ship to prepare to do her sunrise salutations and meditation. It did not matter what planet she was on. She knew it had all been created by the ONE Source. She knew she was that Source; it was in her being. This beautiful Source was in all things. She would take her time and do the rituals she usually did on her home planet. She set her intent to ground herself with the planet Earth as she usually did on her planet Mentaka. She then rolled her mat out onto the ground and sat down crossing one leg over the other. She quieted her mind, taking in several deep breaths. In her mind's eye, she felt all of nature was nearby her. She joined with them in her mind and became one with them as they journeyed through the forest. Several hours had past and now A'na must go back into the ship and do the investigative work she thought would provide the answers she needed. That evening while she did her meditation she would again connect telepathically with her family, letting her loved ones back on Mentaka know she was safe.

The next thing she needed to do was to thoroughly check each one of the ship's energetic crystals. The crystals were responsible for the working energy of the whole ship and its systems operations. She already had a sick feeling in her gut, it was the crystals. She carefully and slowly opened the latch door and removed the first crystal. It was so beautiful! It is a huge, clear, and bright quartz crystal weighing about twenty pounds.

She took it out into the sunshine where she could get a good look. Upon her inspection, it was fine, with no cracks or fractures.

It required sunlight as this would only help to keep it charged and so she left it on the ground near the ship. Ten such crystals power the ship, and she would do this for each one of them. The second, third, and fourth crystals were all fine, as was the fifth crystal. The sixth, seventh, and eighth crystals were also fine but, the ninth and tenth crystals were not. The ninth crystal had a fracture that was barely detectable. The tenth crystal, however, had a fracture that had turned into a crack. It is enough to disrupt the correct functioning of the instruments. Enough to take her off track from her coordinates and not sound an alarm for her to hear? She was puzzled. She must be overlooking something. So much for trusting her instruments! For now, she would have to look at the constellations to figure out exactly where she was. Her science training would come in handy. She would have to rely on her knowledge of the stars to find out where she was. Right now, she considered this her most important task to complete but it would have to wait until nightfall and clear skies. She decided to make the most of her day. She would explore her surroundings!

A'na has a curious nature, exploring this new world would be what she considers fun. Fortunately, she has a bag packed with emergency supplies, water, clothes, essential oils, her handheld computer for notes, calculations, etc. She changed into more appropriate clothing and shoes for hiking. The clothing she wears naturally repels any dirt, hair, and moisture. Most all wear a white suit on her planet. It is a relaxed-fitting top and pants, a gauzy type of material that is made from plant materials in her area of the planet. Each area has its own way of doing things, although they are all similar. Her hiking clothes are more appropriate for blending in with her environment. She put on her hiking shoes. They are more cushioned and have a better sole grip than the shoes she had on. She gets her day bag and off she goes into the forest.

A'na has decided she will keep a journal of each day so that she can look back on it and reflect. She dictates in her journal entry, "Day two: A hike in the woods."

A'na is excited to go on this hike and explore a new world and its inhabitants, its terrain, its nature, and learn about it firsthand.

She enters the forest on a little path that has been used by the woodland creatures. As she enters the forest she is again greeted by its inhabitants. They have come to greet her like old friends. She is glad for the company. They walk along the path together as the fairies and nature spirits come along too. It would be quite an unusual sight for someone unfamiliar with A'na's ways, she and about twenty-five creatures walking together through the woods. The creatures are quite happy to have a human friend who can understand them and know what they are thinking, to hear and to care about their concerns, what changes they would like to see take place within the forest they are traveling and their world in general. There is a great concern on the woodland creatures' minds, which they share with A'na. The creatures are aware of what is and has taken place on the planet for many thousands of years. They are ready for a new world. It seems that as all of the fear, anger, and chaos has taken hold for the humans, they too have been victims as a result. Many of the woodland creatures have been shot and killed for no reason, left to die in the woods or the field where they lay. There is no honor for them or their lives. They are glad to be able to tell someone of their plight, for someone to listen to them. A'na is greatly concerned and saddened to hear what they are relaying to her telepathically. There is a great fear among the woodland creatures. They are very angry and saddened. A'na knows she must enter these many concerns in her journal when she gets back to the ship.

The rest of the hike is uneventful and relaxing as she gets a feel of the woods. A'na takes notice of the forest as she continues her journey. There were trees of all sizes and ages. She noticed several older trees as she walked further into the forest. She was deep in the woods and there was a clean, crisp smell to the morning air, something she thought she would be missing. As she walked to the creek, she was aware of the sound that was made as she planted one foot in front of the other on the ground, signaling all the years of fallen leaves beneath her feet. The feel, the smell, and the sounds of nature were there before her eyes and ears, similar to home. Nature is what makes her heart sing, the natural world. The blue sky above was mostly hidden from view by the newly developing canopy of leaves. Rays of sunshine would be allowed to enter the woods intermittently, providing an aura of mystery that only invited A'na to go further into the forest towards the creek. This is a time that would allow her to completely escape any thoughts of her predicament. She realized that her surroundings possess a beauty, not unlike her home planet, Mentaka. As A'na and the woodland creatures go deeper into the forest she feels the air become cooler. She hears the trickle of the creek, and she sees the dark green moss on the creek banks, the color of emeralds. The creek was making gurgling sounds that seemed to call out her name. She walked down a slight incline through a thick jumble of fallen trees and overgrowth. There she is surrounded by several dogwood trees and smaller bushes by the creek. The woods were speckled with many shades of color. She took notice of the moss growing on an old oak tree. It was almost blue with hints of gray and brown blended into the edges, darker brown flecks scattered all around its surface. Deer moss was scattered here and there. There was a fallen tree laying across the creek with many shades of gray. Its center, almost black with the color fading to soft shades of silver at the furthest tips. Its surface is worn smooth from the heavy traffic of woodland creatures using it as a bridge to cross the creek. A'na stops for a moment to ponder on Mentaka, the home she loves so much. She takes in a big breath and imagines she is there by her waterfall pool. She allows herself to be there in her mind. This comforts A'na and makes her feel extremely happy as she misses the sounds of her watery planet. The creek is just a small trickling sound compared to the often heard "roar" of the waterfall, but it is live water. This is a sound that both relaxes and energizes A'na. A smile is on her face as she takes off her hiking shoes for a walk in the creek! As she steps into the water, she feels a mushiness beneath her feet. She is aware that under the surface of sand and leaves there is a silty mess of more decayed leaves and dirt. It was not the firm sand and small massaging pebbles in the waters' floor she was used to.

After her little walk in the creek, A'na finds a big rock on which to sit and enjoy the water and fruit she had brought for the hike. While sitting on this rock she reflects upon her world with gratitude and joy. She knows she is fortunate to have lived in such a wonderfully magical place as Mentaka. She has lived on many planets and in many places as she remembers and knows each one. She has, however lived upon planet Earth in earlier historic times. She misses her planet Mentaka, and it has only been two days. Her mind wanders, about how long she will be here, and somewhere in the back of her mind, she wonders if she will get back to Mentaka. She also knows in her heart that there are no mistakes in life, only life lessons. The Universe conspires to inspire. She will follow her spiritual heart and listen to her gut. She knows that she is there for a reason. She will just have to be patient until that time.

She returned to her ship in time for her sunset meditation with the nature creatures nearby. After nightfall, she lay a blanket on the ground so that she could lie there and stare up at the stars and look for familiar constellations or constellations she could recognize. She could then enter the constellations into her journal and know without doubt where exactly where she was in the Milky Way and maybe exactly where she was on the planet Earth. She saw several constellations in the sky that she recognized. Earth, as most all planets have come and gone, come and been rebirthed several times, going through times of higher consciousness and lower consciousness. There had been times of light and times of darkness. This present time was the beginning of a time of great change, and she knew that this meant a time of great chaos and confusion. Things would be shaken up and rearranged as Mother Earth cleansed herself in preparation for her ascension. She did not want to interfere in a world that was going through such change. But yet, she knew she was here on planet Earth for a purpose, and she knew in her heart that purpose would be revealed to her at the right moment. She just had to believe and allow things to play out. She also knew that others from other planets had already interfered many thousands of years ago and they would be on the ready to do so again if possible. But on the other hand, there were those extraterrestrials that had help to "seed" the planet Earth and would be coming to assist their "families" into the light of a new way of living and existing.

Each day A'na dictated to her journal before going to sleep and each morning she would go on a hike with the nature creatures. She goes a little further out each day. On the third week, she feels she is going to meet someone. She intends to go out further and asks the creatures to stay in hiding for their safety. She is very careful not to let herself be seen until she knows for sure what she is dealing with.

She walks a great deal further into a small populated area where she sees several humans. She quickly darts behind a tree so as not to be seen by anyone. She observes their behavior for quite some time and concludes that they are about to have others join them for a celebration of some type. It appears that there is food that has been prepared and is sitting on a table outside. There are several chairs. She observes a round object with tiny candles on top. She is not familiar with this object. A'na has never had sugar that has been manmade and processed. There is no processed food on Mentaka, only what is grown. It has different colors on the very top and it is placed in the center of one of the tables. Beside this object are five boxes of different sizes that are wrapped in different types of colored paper and have bows on them. She remembers they are called presents, or gifts. A'na is familiar with gifts but not the colored paper on them. There are many translucently colored bags of air tied throughout the area. She is not familiar with balloons. There is the sound of music playing. Soon several other adult humans join outside where several older children are gathered. A'na is so curious and decides to come in closer for a better look. As she repositions herself, she sees that one of the older children seems to be looking her way. A'na quickly stands still and then peeks to see if she is still being noticed. What she doesn't know is that this older child has mentioned to another girl that she saw a woman in the woods. When A'na comes out from behind the tree a young girl is standing there looking at her! A'na is startled by the girl and has many thoughts going through her mind. She is not afraid of the girl, but she must come up with a storyline in which to tell her and the other people that will not scare them.

"Who are you?" asks the girl. "My name is Lucy. Did you come to join the party?" A'na tells the young girl her name is A'na and explains she has just been hiking in the woods when she noticed their house. "This is my birthday party, although it is not my real birthday." explains the young girl. A'na nodded at Lucy with a look of puzzlement on her face. "My real birthday is on December 24th," says Lucy as she takes A'na by the hand and leads her to the party and begins introducing her to the others and her mother. They each say hello to A'na as they snicker and laugh. Her mother says hello to A'na as she pulls Lucy to the side and asks, "Aren't you a little old to be having invisible friends?" Lucy looks at her mother with a look of shock on her face. She insists that her friend is right there in front of their eyes. Lucy feels so embarrassed and humiliated as she runs back towards the woods with tears in her eyes. She is obviously upset. A'na is right behind her. A'na processes the situation very quickly and wants to explain it to Lucy in a way that she too, will understand. Lucy is crying and is upset that everyone thinks she is playing a joke and pretending to have a new friend. A'na leans down and takes Lucy by the hand. She begins by asking

Lucy not to cry and explains to her that evidently, only she can see her. Lucy does not understand at all and is quite astonished by what A'na has just said. She stopped crying long enough to say, "I don't understand. How can I see you and they can't?" asks Lucy. A'na has to explain this to Lucy in such a way that Lucy can understand what is happening, as many adults would not begin to understand it, only a few on the planet may know, and understand what has just taken place.

"Lucy, please keep an open mind as I try to explain all of this to you. I don't want to scare you," exclaimed A'na. I have come here by accident from another planet. I am what most of the people on your planet would call an extraterrestrial or alien. I am not from planet Earth. Please do not be afraid. I am not here to harm you or anyone. I am temporarily lost, and my spacecraft needs some repair work. It may take me some time to repair my ship. To be honest, the fact is, you are very special, Lucy. Only you can see me because of several reasons, your spiritual heart is open and you have a higher vibration than most other people on your planet at this time. You have a heart filled with love and an open mind. Your eyes can see me, the others cannot. Also, my body is not as dense as your body because I am from a different dimension. It just means that I am a bit less opaque than you are here on your planet Earth. It is just one of our differences. To Lucy, she appeared to be a tall and beautiful woman with a kind face and voice to match.

Lucy was quiet for several minutes. She did not seem shaken or scared. To be honest, Lucy felt so very close to A'na when she first laid eyes upon her. She could not help herself but come closer. She was drawn to A'na like a magnet or a moth to the light. She explained this to A'na. Lucy told A'na she just felt better when she came closer to her. She could not explain it. A'na knew this girl was an old soul who was aware of life on a different level than those of her peers, adults included. She hugged Lucy and reassured her they were friends. She advised Lucy to collet herself and she encouraged Lucy to go back to the house and the party and to act as if nothing had happened. A'na promised Lucy she would see her the next day at 10am in the same woods by the creek. But, before they departed, A'na asked Lucy; 'What is the name of your planet? Lucy replied: "Earth." A'na asked, "What year is it, Lucy?" Lucy replied: "2022." "Lucy, what is the name of your area?" inquired A'na. Lucy seemed puzzled as she looked at A'na. "I am not sure what you are asking me. We are in Statesville, North Carolina. We are in the United States of America," Lucy replied with uncertainty. It was just as the woodland creatures had told A'na, planet Earth. Had she wanted it to be a different planet she had landed on? She knew in her mind she was exactly where she was supposed to be. There are no accidents! The Universe always conspires to inspire. She just needed to flow with her circumstances and see where they would lead her. It was obvious Lucy was part of this plan.

A'na was so very excited to see humans even if they could not see her. It confirmed what the woodland creatures had told her and what she already thought to be true. Why was she having doubts about what the woodland creatures had already told her? A'na was aware that she really had not been her true self since landing. She was not sure why. She had to reassure herself she was fine and all was good. She had to trust the process. She had not been challenged in her beliefs in so long. Why should she have any doubt now. BELIEVE she told herself, BELIEVE. There are no accidents! She would finish her calculations from her constellation notes this evening and then she could confirm her exact location. A'na had a skip in her walk and a warmth in her heart as she reflected upon meeting the girl, Lucy. She had a very special place in A'na's heart already. She was not sure exactly why, but it didn't matter. A'na loved children. She loved all. She knew no other way but to love and respect all. She saw beyond what the eyes can see. She felt the genuine love this child possessed, her compassion, and her concern for others. What she didn't know was how close they would become. She was not prepared for the love she would experience for this young girl named Lucy.

As A'na walked back deeper into the woods she came across her animal friends, the woodland creatures. Together they walked back to A'na's ship as she relayed her story of meeting Lucy and told them about the others not being able to see her. The woodland creatures were not surprised by this as most of the humans had a type of amnesia. They were not aware of a lot of things! The woodland creature was far more aware of everything than most of the humans.

A'na felt a sense of relief in many ways; if they could not see her, they could not see her spacecraft either. It would give her another layer of protection for now and keep her presence from interfering in the goings-on of their world at this time. It would keep her from being invaded with questions and possibly harmed. It would also keep her from interfering in the lives of many, causing more fear and chaos at this very shaky time. It just was not the right moment to let her presence be known.

Meanwhile, Lucy went back to the house and the party. She tried to pretend that nothing special was going on, but in her mind, what had just happened was so special she wanted to yell it from the rooftop. She had met a special new friend who made her feel loved and accepted just as she is. Lucy felt a level of closeness and comfort the moment she laid eyes on A'na and not only that, A'na was from another planet! Lucy had to pinch herself to make sure she wasn't dreaming. She hummed and skipped most of the rest of the day. As she went to bed that night, she had so many thoughts and questions going through her mind that she couldn't sleep. She was so very excited and could not wait until 10am. She knew she had to calm down and not call any further attention to her unusual happiness, but it was difficult to do. It was Spring but there was not any school due to the pandemic. She would be in the tenth grade if she got to go back to school this season. She stayed home alone for most of the time while her mom and dad worked on and off. She had a neighbor that could come and check on her from time to time or if needed.

Lucy was the youngest of three children, the others were grown and out of the house. Her brothers and sisters were married with children of their own. Lucy has nieces and nephews her age. She often had to explain this to the other kids in school as they did not understand how that could be. Her parents were much older than the other parents. She felt like an only child. She was on her own much of the time on the small farm that her parents owned. She spent a lot of time out of doors in the woods and with her animal friends. She knew she was somehow different than most of the other kids and her family. She wasn't exactly sure how she was different. She was more tender hearted and sensitive in many ways. Someday she would know and understand why.

The pandemic had taken a toll on everyone. In the past, Lucy's house and yard would have been filled with people at the party laughing and having a good time. Family and friends would be playing their instruments and singing. It is different now because of the pandemic. Most everyone was afraid of getting sick and dying. Many people had died, and families could not go to the funeral. Lucy knew many things had changed. She and her family no longer went to visit friends and much less time was being spent with her brother and sisters and their families. She did not get to spend time playing with her cousins, or her nieces and nephews. Friends were no longer allowed to come and visit.

Life was so very different. Sometimes she felt very sad. Parts of the planet were on fire, other parts of the country and the world were fighting the pandemic, hospitals were turning patients away. She knew children were dying from the pandemic. People were not working. Many had lost their jobs. Prices were inflated on many items and groceries were in short supply. Lucy was only twelve, but even she knew that her world seemed to be in trouble. She was so happy to have met A'na. Lucy had wanted to help her world in some way but was not sure what a child of twelve could do to make a difference. She thought that maybe A'na could help her.

That night as A'na lay under the stars she thought about Lucy. She thought about what and how she was going to explain her world on a 5th-dimensional planet. What it is like and why it was so different from her planet. She wanted to give Lucy the answers she was looking for without confusing her. She wanted to give her an understanding of what it is like living on a 5th-dimensional planet and why it was this way. After all, her planet was going to be a 5th-dimensional planet in the very near future. She decided that Lucy was no different than one of her students and she would teach her and share many things with her, that is if she wished to know more. She knew Lucy would be able to do some miraculous things in her life and she was excited to be a part of Lucy's journey into expanded consciousness.

Chapter 6

Mentaka 101

It was a little before 10am and Lucy decided to head into the woods to meet A'na at the creek where they would get to know each other a little better. Just as she said, A'na was waiting on Lucy. Some of the woodland creatures were there with her. Lucy assured the creatures she would not harm them. Lucy was aware of the woodland creatures coming in closer. She loved the creatures and wanted to help them in any way she could. It was a wonderful feeling for Lucy, being so close to the woodland creatures, close enough to touch them, to feel their beauty and have their trust in such a significant way. She knew exactly why the creatures trusted A'na, they, just as she, felt her love, her kindness, and her big generous heart. They too felt A'na's pure love and acceptance. There was no need for fear.

It was a beautiful spring day. The birds were singing, and the creek was happily trickling along. The wind offered gentle breezes and hints of wildflower blossoms filled the air. All of the woodland creatures made themselves comfortable and sat by A'na and Lucy. They would alert A'na if they heard anyone coming. A'na still had some fruit from Mentaka and shared it with Lucy who ate all that she had brought to the creek. A'na also brought a jug of water from her planet and asked Lucy if she would like a drink. Lucy drank a few sips and then she asked A'na; "Why does your water taste so different?" A'na asked; "What do you mean?" Lucy explained that it tasted so much better than the water she drank from their well, but that she could not explain what she meant. It was just better than the water she had been drinking all her life. A'na knew the answer but kept it to herself for now, for the present moment. She sensed that Lucy was aware of many things!

Lucy looked at the fruit and saw many different fruits than what she was familiar with. There were fruits that looked like giant grapes and tasted like grapes. She tried one fruit that looked like an orange but had the texture of a banana, with the taste of an apple. Hmmm, she thought. Once Lucy had finished eating some of the fruits they just walked and played in the creek splashing each other and having fun. The sun peeked through the trees as the morning light danced on their leaves. Lucy and A'na came back to the sandy area to dry off and just relax. A'na had brought a blanket for them to sit upon. It was made from the same gauzy material as the clothes A'na wore. Lucy noticed it repelled the sand. She also noticed that it dried within moments of being wet. The blanket was in multiple layers of material for comfort. It felt soft and comfy and was weightless but felt thick at the same time. The blanket only made Lucy even more curious about the planet A'na lived on, but she had to ask A'na, "How did you get here on planet Earth? Lucy, she replied. "It was my turn to go out and do our border watch. I was almost finished when I decided to take a quick nap and fell deeply asleep. When I woke up after landing, I had not landed on Mentaka but was on planet Earth. It seems I have a fracture in two of the crystals that propel the ship. I need to replace or repair them before I am space-bound again. They are rather large, clear, quartz crystals" "Oh, said Lucy. What will you do?" Not to worry, Lucy, an answer will come. I have faith and believe all things and circumstances happen for a reason. In the meantime, I will get to know you and planet Earth a little bit more.

In the back of Lucy's mind, she wanted to see A'na's space spacecraft! She wondered what it looked like, what it is made of, how big it is. She wondered if she could ride in it. She was full of questions but held her questions about the ship for later. She just didn't think it was the time to ask those questions of A'na.

Lucy looked at A'na and asked: "Could you tell me everything about your planet?" A'na looked at Lucy and asked: "Where shall I begin?" Lucy said, "Tell me everything, every detail. I want to know everything about your planet and your life." A'na took in a big breath and let out a sigh. She was so glad to hear that Lucy wanted to know everything and she was excited to tell her. A'na thought for a moment, "Hmmm, where do I begin, she pondered?"

She decided to tell Lucy about the physical description of her planet first. As you know, my planet is called Mentaka. We are also located in the Milky Way star system, but we are on the fringes at the opposite end of the Milk Way from Earth. It is a very, very old planet. Planet Earth will have not any recognition or history of my planet Mentaka, as it does not exist in your time, your reality. I live in one of the most beautiful areas of Mentaka, it is what you would call a coastal climate. We have tropical plants but do not have the hot, humid temperature you experience in most of your tropical areas. The area of the planet I live on stays very comfortable at 70 to 75 degrees. We get light rains every three days or so. There is always a gentle breeze blowing. My planet is very watery. It has many waterfalls, and pools that were formed by the waterfalls. The pool water is always warm, around 84 degrees because of the geothermal springs that run under it. It is a beautiful aqua blue turning a deeper shade of blue as the water gets deeper. We have beautiful plants, ferns, flowers, and trees. We have lots of creeks, streams, and springs. The springs are considered to be very healing and it is a nice place to gather and to soak in the restorative waters. There is a clay present in the geothermal springs that when used on the body it is very cleansing and moisturizing. There are eight oceans on Mentaka. We also have a very special and sacred cave which is in the area I call home. It is located behind one of the waterfalls. It is called "The Cave of Rebirth," I will have to tell you more about this sacred cave a bit later. As I mentioned, our planet is located on the other side of the Milky Way constellation. We have one sun and two moons. Lucy had a very puzzled look on her face. "A'na what do you mean when you say that Mentaka does not exist in our time? Is it not the same or close to the same time on your planet as it is here on Earth?" asked Lucy. A'na looked at Lucy and said I promise I will explain this to you, but it may take a while as there is much to tell and share with you about my planet Lucy." A'na explained. Lucy nodded and agreed. "Wow!" said Lucy.

You see Lucy on the planet where I come from, Mentaka, it is both mystical and magical. I think the word your planet would use to describe my planet Mentaka is "enchanted." We are not born into the "duality" that your planet is, thinking we are separate from our Source. Lucy looked at A'na with an expression of complete puzzlement on her face. "What is duality?" "What is Source?" she asked A'na. Lucy I am going to be explaining many different terms and definitions to you, but for the most part it is related to how we experience our reality. We experience a different reality from you. We know and understand that everything is connected and originating from the same Source. Source is the ONE that created everything in the known Universe. I believe one of the terms you use on planet Earth for our Source is GOD, or Allah. You have what is referred to as the "Good Book," which describes some of the events that have led to certain beliefs on your planet. It was written by men and women who have written what they interpreted GOD to be telling them. In other words, the words were passed through the perspective of the recipient that was writing what they thought was being said. Lucy said, "Yes you are referring to the Bible." Our knowledge on Mentaka is known as we are born. We have a broader understanding of our lives, where we originate from and what you would refer to as our past, present and future lives. Our reality is in the 5th dimension. and Earth, at the present moment, is in the third dimension, mainly, although you have some who are experiencing fourth and fifth- dimensional reality. Dimensions vibrate at different rates of speed. That is why your family and friends could not see me at your birthday party. The 3rd dimension vibrates much slower than those who are experiencing a 5th dimensional reality. Most of your inhabitants on Earth are still very much asleep, as we say, and are not aware of life other than what is before their eyes. It is not that my planet is better. Our reality is different than yours. We, all of us, including you and the inhabitants of Earth are eternal light beings at our core, as are all of the creations of our Source. We, all of us are of what you call, God's creations, originating from the other side of "the veil," but each one of us is on a different journey and path. While you may think of yourself as an individual while in your 3rd dimensional body, it is but an illusion. Your soul is experiencing what you need at this time, in this lifetime. Your planet, Earth is mystical and magical too, it is just that most of the people are not aware of it, not aware that your planet, Mother Earth is a consciousness too, as are the oceans, the air, the sky, the sun, and the moon and all of nature. All of creation is created by the same Source and all are connected and communicating in some kind of way. What may make our planet seem more magical is that we are able to see the creatures and beings that are "caretakers" of the air, water, plants and etc. You see Lucy, life is there before us in different layers. There is layer, upon layer, upon layer, and dimension, upon dimension. You are but a facet of the many parts of your being.

Lucy, you had asked me earlier about the reason the water I brought from Mentaka tasted soooo good, it is because it is infused with Divine Love. On Mentaka, our life is based on the knowledge of our origins, that of Divine Love from our Source. We know in our spiritual heart that this Source is always within our being. It is known before birth and reinforced after our birth into the physical. Our whole planet exists with this vibration and knowing. All are respected, loved, and honored, that includes the planet, the air, the moon and the stars, the plants, the insects, the animals, the waters, and all of her inhabitants, including the "caretakers." The vibration of unconditional love is a high vibration that can be infused into everything! It can be infused into food, plants, crystals, water, ice, snowflakes, everything, even on your planet. It is done with intention. The vibration of unconditional love becomes a part of the object that is being infused. It is not only on my planet but all over the Universe where there is intention to do so. We will talk about the act of intention a little later.

A'na was so very excited to share everything with Lucy. She told Lucy that she too has had many other lives and journeys, not just this life on Earth she is aware and living now. It is call reincarnation. There are those on your planet that believe in reincarnation and those that think it is not possible, not real. Remember Lucy, we are eternal beings of light. On the other side of the veil, we are in an ocean of consciousness. We are the drops of the ocean as well as being the ocean. Lucy, know this, if you can imagine it so, it can become so. You are capable of so much more than you believe yourself to be. When you are ready you will know this for yourself. You will become the master of your life! God is within you as you are an extension of our SOURCE.

Lucy was busy imagining Mentaka as A'na continued with her description of the planet. She could see Mentaka in her mind's eye, and all of the beauty surrounding it as A'na was describing each and every detail, including her spiritual beliefs. Lucy felt as if she were in a dream as A'na was describing her life and her planet. It seemed familiar, almost like she had been there before. She would love to live on a planet like Mentaka. Lucy was soaking in all of A'na's descriptions of Mentaka and its' people in her little mind. She wanted to know more. Lucy asked A'na, "Do you live in houses?" A'na said: "Yes, but they are not houses like you live in. We live in houses if we choose, many prefer to live in nature with huts, or a lean-to that is made from grasses. I live in a crystal house that I share with my extended family members some of the time. We have many, many crystals on my planet and they are used in many different ways. I often prefer to sleep out in the open under the stars, to be out in nature. Compared to life on Earth it is a very simple life, but also a very happy and uncomplicated life. We live with great purpose. We interact with all of nature on a daily basis. Life is easy and there is a genuine feeling of unconditional love and respect between all. We spend much time in meditation, sending love and light to and throughout the entire Universe.

Lucy, I want you to know that you will have many more visitors coming to Mother Earth in the near future to help in your transition in becoming a fifth-dimensional planet. Your patience and knowledge will be needed for the people of your planet, to assure them, and to let them know of things that are happening and why. Your planet has been protected for a long time now. It was done to keep those out who had done harm and damage in the past. Your planet is always on everyone's radar. Earth is considered one of the most beautiful and diverse planets in the Milky Way. Your planet is considered a planet of hard knocks. You are greatly respected because of it, living life in a 3rd dimensional reality is not easy. What goes on here on planet Earth is of great interest to many. You have a collection of interesting DNA on your planet. Many of your people have multidimensional or galactic blood in their DNA. This information is not known on your planet at this time, but it will become known in your future.

So naturally, your galactic family is interested in what goes on here. There are many ships around your atmosphere watching and maintaining guard over your planet as we speak. I must have gone through unnoticed or "allowed" to enter.

Lucy was very astonished by what A'na had just told her, and she had to ask, "A'na do you mean that I may have ancestors from another planet?" A'na looked at Lucy with a puzzled grin and said, "Yes, most everyone does, including me and you." "Well, why would I have DNA in my blood from other planets? What planets are you referring to?" Lucy asked. I will name a few of them for you, Lucy. Some of the planets are Venus, Arcturus, Pleiades, Orion, and Mentaka of course. I will tell you this briefly. Your planet was an experiment of sorts. Many came to Earth long ago and some did terrible things to the humans and her inhabitants. Some came as seed bearers to have inhabitants on the planets. Some came after that for self-gain. This was long, long ago. We are all seeing the best outcome for planet Earth and know it is to be so. It is talked about in the channels of history. I know it may seem hard to believe any of this from what you have been told and what beliefs you may hold as your own, but just try to be open and allow this information to pass through to your brain. I imagine it is quite confusing, all of the many things I am sharing with you and telling you about. Just let this information sit with you a bit.

Some of the other planets and their inhabitants are not in a fifth-dimensional consciousness either and would rather see things happen that would benefit themselves. Your planet is already destined to win the battle between light and dark and the light will win this battle. Your Mother Earth will ascend and those who wish to ascend with her are welcome. Your world will be a joyous place and your life will be different and so will those who have chosen to ascend. Lucy stopped A'na she did not know what the word ascension meant and wanted to know more. A'na agreed she would explain what ascension meant but she would like to wait until she explained some other things first. She felt it would make much more sense. Lucy nodded her head in agreement.

Getting back to Mentaka. We do not have the places you do with all kinds of clothes, gadgets, and things. We do not shop in stores. We do not have stores. We do not have a monetary system. We do not have laws or jails, or prisons. This type of thing is not needed on our planet as we all have the same consciousness, wanting the same thing, of unconditional love and respect. We have open-air markets and mainly trade and or barter for things we may need in our daily lives. We do not spend our days working in jobs we do not care for. Our days are filled with joy. We take time to be grateful and enjoy our lives, finding happiness in every second. Most of our supplies are very minimal and are created by using thought and energy. Lucy, had to stop A'na before she went any farther. "What do you mean supplies are created by using thought and intent"? "Do you just think about something and it appears?" Lucy inquired. "Well not exactly, you have to remember that our consciousness is in a different reality and therefore our thought patterns are different, our needs are different because of this. We do use our energy, combined with our thoughts and our intent to bring about certain things. We can see them as being so and so they are." explained A'na. The mana that I had mentioned earlier is part of the energy that is on our planet. We absorb this energy into our vessels, and it provides sustenance for our bodies.

Lucy wanted to know more about this "mana." "What does mana look like? She asked A'na. "It is like little squiggly things in the air that are filled with light, life giving light." A'na explained. Hmm, Lucy thought to herself. I would really like to see it, she said aloud.

A'na continued with her description of life on Mentaka. We do not have automobiles either. We use our hovercrafts that are powered by crystals if needed for transportation. We do not have televisions or the internet. We have a library, but it is one that we enter through our meditation. We can download information into our minds similar to your computer downloads. We can see the information in our minds.

We do not have a need for items to entertain ourselves, other than the need for art. That would include pottery, paintings, and other art forms, as well as music and musical instruments. Aesthetics and the appreciation of beauty are very much a part of our culture. All of our musical instruments are handcrafted by very well-trained artisans. Dance is also a large part of our lives. We are out in nature most of the time. We enjoy spending our time in productive ways and meditating for long periods, teaching, sharing our time, and being with our loved ones and others. We have gardens for vegetables, and we take care of the gardens together. There is no such thing as hunger or starvation. It is always a community garden, and all is shared by everyone. The weather is temperate. It is always a comfortable 70 to 74 degrees in my area of the planet. Some of the outer regions have a different climate and some regions even have snow. I have visited these regions before and have seen a variety of different animals than what I am used to. The snow was very beautiful, as well as the snow creatures that this climate supports. It is less populated. For me, I prefer the temperate climate. There is something for all to enjoy on the planet.

We place our respect for our love of Source and all living things first and foremost in our lives. All are treated like family. We have different sexes, men and women. We also have those who are androgynous, being partly male and partly female in appearance, of indeterminate sex. We can choose to take a mate or not. We can choose to remain without a mate. It is our choice, a choice that each individual makes, their choice is respected. We have lots of children on our planet and we all love and cherish them, taking care of them as if they are our own. We have romantic love but mainly the love that we share, that is always present, is more a love of respect and honor for one another, unconditional love.

Again, Lucy says: "WOW!" as she imagined herself lying there under the stars at night with A'na by her side as A'na continued with her detailed description of Mentaka. Lucy asked: "Could you please tell me more about your crystal house. Can you see through it? Is it clear?" A'na laughed and said: "It is not clear enough to see through it, but it is opaque. It is translucent and the light rushes through it, making small rainbows in each of the rooms. We do not have what you call kitchens as we only eat raw fruits and veggies. We drink a lot of water. It is always available in special hydrants. It is pumped into the hydrants through a special alloy or material that is anti-bacterial and antimicrobial. There is not any illness or disease on my planet. We do not have doctors or hospitals. We have an herbal specialist who can recommend herbs if they are needed. Lucy had a concerned look on her face. She said: "Don't you get hungry?" "Not really," A'na replied. It is a way of life on my planet, and this is how we are brought up. We are not used to bringing much food into our bodies. We get much of our energy and sustenance from the Mana in the air or from our light within. "Mana? What is Mana?" Lucy asked. That would be a difficult question for A'na to answer without going into some of the other areas she will be sharing with Lucy. For now, she just answered, "It is energy."

A'na knew the day had passed quickly and thought she needed to send Lucy back home. She assured Lucy they would meet at the same time and place tomorrow and they would continue their discussion of Mentaka. After Lucy headed towards home, A'na continued to sit and relax by the creek and telepathically talked with her woodland friends. The creatures loved having A'na there with them. It offered a security they had not known in their time on planet Earth. There had been tales passed down that it was not always that way. It has been told that in ancient times the woodland creatures interacted with humans for a great period in time. A'na assured them it would be that way again someday. It gave the creatures hope for a better tomorrow. As A'na walked back to her ship with her woodland friends she checked in with the Mother tree and all the other trees nearby. All was good. It was a good day. She had not felt the pings of missing her planet so much while telling Lucy about it and she loved having Lucy and the woodland creatures nearby. She knew she was there for a reason and if for nothing else she enjoyed giving hope to the woodland creatures and sharing her planet's story and beliefs with Lucy.

Before she had gotten back to the ship, her thoughts had already shifted to the fractured crystals. She knew even when she got her exact location, she could not send the info out into space to her home planet to assure them of her safety. She needed to have all ten crystals in place and working order. She would be stranded on planet Earth until she repaired or replaced the two fractured crystals. She continued to have the crystals lay in the sun for the energy they needed, but the sun would not repair a fractured crystal. She needed to replace it or repair it another way, but with what crystal and where? She knew she would figure it out. In the meantime, she would make the most of the situation and work with Lucy, all the while reminding herself there are no mistakes. She knew deep in her heart that she was meant to be here at this time in this location. She just didn't know why, at least for now. It would be revealed to her at the right time. She continued to dictate to her journal, noting her time spent with Lucy by the creek describing Mentaka with her woodland friends nearby.

Day two with Lucy's Class

As she prepared for the second day with A'na, Lucy went over everything that she had been told thus far about Mentaka. She was intrigued and fascinated. She was a very intelligent girl and she wanted to know more. Today, she brought fruit for her and A'na to enjoy, although it would not be as good as the fruit and water A'na had brought yesterday, but she brought water along too. Lucy was delighted to have a new friend and to be learning something new about a planet far, far, away. She found herself constantly thinking about all that A'na had shared with her, the planet Mentaka and her spiritual beliefs. Although A'na's beliefs were so different than Lucy's beliefs, they seemed to offer her a comfort she had not known.

As she entered the woods, she heard a bird singing and chirping. She looked up and found herself talking to the bird as if it could understand what she was saying. It was a Blue Jay. Just as she walked by, another jay landed nearby. She thought to herself that they must be building a nest. Lucy continued on the path to the creek. She had so many thoughts going through her head as A'na appeared from out of nowhere. They gently hugged each other in a warm welcome and headed closer to the creek. A'na had already laid out the blanket for them to sit upon. Lucy began with many questions. She wanted to know why Mentaka was so different from Earth. She asked A'na why did the creatures trust her and how did she talk with them without talking. She wanted to know more about the crystal home of A'na' lived in. She was giddy with excitement and could not wait to learn more from A'na.

A'na explained to Lucy it would take time to tell her everything about her planet, Mentaka. She told Lucy she would have to be patient as she would explain it all in due time. She thought she would answer the easy questions first, but there was not an easy answer as her questions deserved honest and detailed answers. For now, she answered the questions as best she could. She began by explaining that she talked with the woodland creatures telepathically. Lucy was familiar with the term and knew it meant with her mind, but how could she do that with the woodland creatures or anybody for that matter, Lucy thought. A'na continued, as I use my intent and raise my vibration, I am one with nature and with my fellow humans. I can see your thoughts in my mind, but I would not "listen" if it were not directed to me. On my planet, Mentaka, that is how we communicate, telepathically. We are taught to respect others' private thoughts, but we are also taught to be mindful of the thoughts that we have. We can use our voices at any time and often do so by singing. Singing keeps our vocal cords in shape. It is a good exercise. "Can you sing one of your songs for me to hear?" asked Lucy. "Of course, Lucy." as A'na began to sing a beautiful tune that captured Lucy's heart. The woodland creatures came in closer. It reminded Lucy of the Celtic music she loved to listen to. Ana's singing voice was indescribable. A'na had what Lucy thought was described as perfect pitch. Lucy thought A'na had the voice of an angel from above. She sang soprano, but she could also sing with deep and full tones that gave Lucy chills up her spine. Her singing voice brought the forest alive, as the birds flew in closer, and the woodlands creatures doubled in size. Lucy quietly observed and listened. She too, was mesmerized!

A'na saw and heard the excitement in Lucy's voice as she asked to know more about Mentaka. A'na was pleased she wanted to know more. As for your question about our crystal homes, she began by explaining that Mentaka had many crystals of all sizes and colors, from very, very, big to tiny. They too have a consciousness. She explained that the crystals were used for many things on her planet and that their energy could be directed. Lucy asked: "What kind of energy?" Lucy was drawn to crystals here on planet Earth and had a small collection of them in her room. She would hold them in her hand and look at them at length, but she was not aware of any energy. She just knew she liked them. A'na told Lucy that everything is energy! We will get into crystals and their properties a little later, I promise. Crystal knowledge is one of my favorite subjects!

Chapter 7

Everything is Energy!

Lucy, I am going to be sharing many things with you, for now, we are going to learn a little about energy. I am aware that on your planet right now is a man who has made some very interesting highlights about the energy I am referring to. He is sharing it with your world. I will try to paraphrase what he has to say. He says that we (you) live in a universe of energy and that this energy is constant, incapable of being created or destroyed, and that it can only change from one state to another. The common forms of energy that you recognize from science classes include solid mass or a non-solid matter, such as heat, electrical, sound gravitational, potential (stored energy), and kinetic energy (energy in motion). He goes on to explain, "Quantum physics states that all mass and energy are interchangeable and consequently that mass is merely a manifestation of energy." "Lucy, do you know what this means?" asked A'na. "No," Lucy said while shaking her head back and forth. "I do not." It means that everything, including humans, is simply stored energy in mass particle form. He says that all theories associated with the universal energy field, all matter and psychological processes this includes thoughts, emotions, and beliefs, and attitudes are composed of energy. Think about this, Lucy. When this theory is applied to your human body, every atom, every molecule, cell tissue, and system, the body is composed of energy that when superimposed on each other creates what is known as the human energy field. So Lucy, let's simplify. Everything is energy in various forms. The sustenance I mentioned earlier, mana, is another form of energy. We breathe it into our bodies, and it provides us with life-giving sustenance. It is in the air that we breathe. The ONE also created the air we breathe, that you breathe, that the plants and animals breathe.

"Lucy, I know this is a lot for you to take in. I hope that this answers your question about mana on Mentaka. It is alright if this is too much information to take in now. Keep these notes and the recording of it and let it sink in when it will." said A'na matter-of-factly. It is very important that you know and understand what is being said. It may take some time. What A'na has shared will allow Lucy to understand the overall connectedness of the Universe. Lucy, I want you to know that we are all connected and communicating with each other, with our bodies, with our organs, with our DNA, and with our cells, and of course, with our consciousness. We are communicating with all of creation in some energetic way! Lucy, please know that this is a subtle world. You have been indoctrinated to believe certain thoughts, which have led you to believe certain things about life, your life, and the general way of things. I know this is all new to you. Wow, Lucy, your thoughts have energy! Thought before form. Lucy, I want you to truly think about this, and let it sit with you. It will make sense, I promise. Happiness is a state of mind.

You have this same person here on your Earth at the present, that is making beautiful discoveries, and he is making others aware of his discoveries. I want to present some more of his discoveries with you so that you can get an idea of what I am and will be discussing with you further. He says that in particle form, the human body is composed of four types of tissues:

epithelial (skin), connective, muscle, and nerve tissue. He says upon closer examination of the epithelial tissue it shows how the tissue is created by these superimposed energy fields. Lucy that is the way of the Universe. It is layer after layer of energy and dimensions. That is why heaven is right here. On my planet and your planet. Heaven is right here. Layer after layer. Dimension after dimension. Heaven is a state of mind.

"Lucy, just let the recorder get this information. It is too much to take down in your handwritten notes. I know that this is a lot of information for you to understand but, someday you will understand completely, what I am sharing with you. It is of grave importance to know this." A'na told her. This has been discovered on your planet Earth. He talks about observing the skin. "Note the wrinkles, the fine hairs, and the nail beds." He asks you to hit a table and hear the sound, to feel how solid it appears to be." He now asks you to magnify the skin under a microscope. He magnified the skin 20,000 times. Now the solid mass of skin turns into a field of swarming cells. He magnifies the skin yet again, the magnification reveals the organelles are composed of molecules. Molecules are created when two or more atoms form chemical bonds with each other. Atoms are building blocks of all matter. A'na continues. There are 90 occurring atoms in the periodic table that combine to make everyday objects in your world, such as a desk, the air, and even the human body. "Lucy, I know this is a little above your understanding, but you will get the gist of what is being said and this will help you to understand the other things I am going to share with you. Please know it is very important," A'na said very firmly. Be sure to record this. Lucy, some on your planet would refer to these discoveries as science, and they are, but who do you think created the science behind the science? Source is the master magician!

As Lucy went home that afternoon, she was shaking her head trying to understand some of what A'na had told her. She thought she kind of got it, but not really. She wondered if what she understood meant that our bodies were not real? She scratched her head in confusion. What is A'na really telling me? What am I supposed to get from this information? The more questions she asked herself the more she seemed to be confused. Hmmm? She was still very excited, and nothing could change that. She loved hearing all that A'na was sharing with her and the time they spent together. She hid her recorder in her desk, knowing she would have to find a better hiding spot soon, and then she had a thought. If they cannot see her, then maybe they cannot hear her words? Lucy shook her head wondering and quickly washed up for dinner.

As A'na and the woodland creatures made their way back through the woods to the spacecraft, A'na found herself full of thoughts as well. She loved that girl like she did her family. She felt protective of her and wanted to help her in any way she could, given the conditions of the world she was living in at present. A'na knew that group consciousness was in place for a reason. It is what allows the beings in a certain dimension to agree on what is accepted within broad group beliefs, it gives an understanding of the environment, languages, definitions, fundamentals, etc. Each individual still uses their own personal perspective and lens to define, describe, and place values on perceived thoughts, and beliefs. Lucy was, in this life, a part of a third-dimensional group consciousness of which was changing this very second. A'na planned to arm Lucy with information so that she could make informed decisions and find her own spiritual truths for herself as she grew older and became an adult on her ever-changing planet. A'na knew she was giving Lucy much information, but felt it was imperative that she do so. She also knew that Lucy would someday use this information to help many. She did not know how long she would be on Earth with Lucy.

The next day, Lucy asked A'na all of the questions that had been bouncing around in her head. A'na, asked Lucy. "Are you telling me that we are not real, just cells bouncing around like the thoughts in my head?" "Well, Lucy, kind of, but not really. What I can tell you is that we are eternal beings of light, all of us, you, me, your family, all of us." We, that is, all that are in a physical vessel are in a "reality" program. We are a focused intent. This is part of the spirit science. Our Source has panned for every little detail. I believe there are many "helpers," angels assisting in all areas of our existence, behind the veil and with our physical vessels, throughout all of creation. There are many, many angels, archangels, ascended masters, beings of light and more helping us in our journeys. I have given you much information and many clues as to our beingness. What do you think? Are we real, you and I? What is real? When you dream is it real? What is real?

Our focused intent depends on the dimension and experience one has designed for oneself before entering into a physical vessel. Lucy, let me ask you this. Have you ever wondered where your mind is located? Your mind, not your brain. I can tell you about our cells and the doctor's work explaining this, but the best way I can explain our focused intent is to share with you how to go within for the answers you seek. And the way you do this is through meditation, relaxing, and silencing the mind. This is when your spiritual heart can speak to you, not in words but in feelings, you will recognize. Your spiritual heart only knows truth!

Lucy had heard about meditation but did not have a firm understanding of it or what it really was. She had seen pictures of people sitting cross-legged with their eyes shut and their hands positioned in a certain way. She had even heard snide remarks and jokes made about meditation. She really didn't know what to expect. Again, her logical mind had taken over and the questions just kept going through, thought, after thought.

Chapter 8

Meditation

A'na felt like she was preparing Lucy for an inauguration. She felt it deep inside herself and although Lucy was young A'na knew in her heart she was ready to hear all that she could share with her to prepare her for what was coming her way, for her and the population of planet Earth. A'na quieted any concerns or worries that she may have had earlier. She knew that meditation could only help Lucy.

Lucy, on Mentaka, meditation is a way of life. We are brought into the practice of meditation by the age of two. I teach meditation to our two-year-olds. I will be teaching you the same way I teach them, but with a lot more information to support meditation. We will begin by teaching you about meditation and we will end with taking you into a guided meditation. The day is young, and the weather is so beautiful. What a great day for your first meditation technique. "What do you think Lucy? Are you ready to try meditation?" asked A'na, enthusiastically.

Lucy, meditation is a practice where an individual uses a technique, such as mindfulness or focusing the mind on a particular object, thought or activity thereby training one's attention and awareness to achieve a mentally clear and emotionally calm, and stable state of mind. Meditation helps to create a positive mood and outlook, self-discipline, healthy sleep patterns, and for some on your planet, increased pain tolerance. It is learning to take control of one's mind and the thoughts that constantly go through your mind.

Are you aware that on your planet Earth, during most of your waking lives your minds are engaged in a continuous internal dialogue? Think about that. That is why the mind is often given the name "monkey brain" on your planet. The dialogue that you play in your minds, along with your perceived meanings and emotions often triggers one thought after the next. You and everyone else do this every day, all day your mind spins stories about your family, your work, (if you were an adult), your health, the mean kid at school, the rude person in the checkout line at your stores. You are most often not even consciously aware of this internal dialogue and yet it is your greatest source of stress in your lives. Wow! Right? People tend to pay more attention to negative happenings in their lives than they do positive things. You get stuck in a loop, in a pattern of negative thinking. It is this negative thinking that puts a damper on your inner light.

Meditation is your best tool to counter those effects. Much more beneficial than the "happy, get well' pill people pop into their mouths on your planet. Meditation will reduce stress and foster positive experiences and intentions. You can then enjoy the peace of the present moment awareness. Your body will respond in kind and your health will be better and better. Pills will be a thing of the past as your own body is the largest pharmacy with everything you may need already supplied. As your Mother Earth changes so will her people and health issues will someday be a thing of your past.

All of the things I have discussed above would suggest a good reason to meditate, don't you think? Most of the people on your planet experience stress and tension on a daily basis. Most have hectic schedules that cause stress, tension, and sometimes pure exhaustion. Now that the pandemic is part of your daily lives it has added stress not only to the adult population but to the young adults and children, as well. This is the stuff that harms your body from the inside out. Lucy, it not only harms the body, but it harms the mind and your quality of life. It is a trickle-down effect. Not only do you suffer but your family and loved ones also suffer when they are stressed.

Lucy had to stop A'na. "Do you mean when I am sad or angry, I am doing harm to my body?" asked Lucy. "Yes, that is exactly what I am saying Lucy," replied A'na. When you have these negative feelings and emotions in your body, the body releases chemicals into the bloodstream. When you feel angry sometimes you may want to hit something. When you are sad, you may cry and not want to be around anyone. When you think about that mean girl at school it may cause you to have a variety of feelings, not good feelings. You have many feelings that you experience every day. Meditation will reduce the negative thoughts and feelings and reduce your response to any of those feelings as well.

Lucy, it may be impossible at this time not to have some of those emotions on a daily basis but when you learn to meditate it can help you to release them and let go of any harmful feelings you are having. I expect there are many people on your planet that are now beginning to meditate on a regular basis and there will be many, many more as they witness and become aware of the benefits of meditation. Meditation is a way to release this tension and stress. It is a perfect way to take a mini vacation without leaving town or costing extra money to do so. With meditation being a part of your daily routine, you can release the tension and stress from your mind and your body. It is a great way to get more energy and focus. Meditation will also help you to alleviate and overcome anxiety, and worry. Meditation relaxes the mind and body and improves your ability to focus the mind. You will be calmer, able to think more clearly, and understand faster what you learn! Meditation will strengthen your inner resolve. You will also learn to gain the ability to be more patient, tolerant, and considerate. Meditation is an exercise that is needed at a time like this on your Earth. Lucy, meditation also strengthens your intuition and helps to develop the ability for constructive and creative thinking. As you can see there are many, many reasons to meditate. And these are just a few of those reasons.

For me, the most important reason to meditate is to communicate with your inner self. Meditation is an inner training method that can get you closer to spiritual awakening and to understanding who you really are. We are so much more than a human body. We are part of the whole. We are part of something greater than ourselves. We are the vessel for the soul to experience physical life. The calmness, inner peace, and inner clarity you experience in meditation will in a short while, affect your whole day, each and every day.

A rested mind dissipates accumulated stress and cultivates a state of restful alertness. Meditation brings a sense of calm and peace to your daily life. Silence is the birthplace of Happiness.

Yes, you could sit and meditate just for the more than appealing physical and mental benefits alone, but, Lucy, the experience of going within is without measure, the best way to bring about the best version of you! People take time for the things they consider important in their life. Lucy, one could make many excuses about taking time/finding time to meditate. Remember, the mind is a vast frontier!

So, Lucy, we have come full circle. Where do you suppose the mind is located? You have a woman on your planet named Evylyn Brodie who has said the mind is located everywhere there is consciousness. Consciousness is in everything. She also indicates that the mind is not limited to the head but to every part of yourself. Your gut may give you your impression of the situation and /or people. For example, "What is your gut reaction?"

When you go to and trust your gut feeling you are going beyond your logical brain and trusting your body's response.

So Lucy, far beyond the health benefits of meditation it is about getting out of your logical brain and stopping the logical thoughts that constantly invade your mind. Making the connection with your Higher Self and those on the other side of the veil is what we want to do and to do this we have to have to be relaxed and silence the monkey brain. Your breathing is the key Lucy! When you concentrate on your breath and you sit in silence, you can just let the thoughts come and let them go, coming back to your breathing. This relaxation is for you and your soul.

"Lucy, would you like to practice a guided meditation?" asked A'na. Lucy gave A'na a smile and nodded in agreement. I will be leading you along the way. This will be fun. Before we begin let us take a little break, drink some water and stretch our legs. Do you have any comments you would like to make or questions you would like to ask? "A'na do you really think I can learn to meditate?" inquired Lucy. "Oh dear one, everyone can learn to meditate," A'na said with the most enthusiasm in her voice. It just gets better and better.

A'na and Lucy took their time drinking water and relaxing by the creek. A'na asked Lucy if she was ready for her first guided meditation. Lucy replied, "YES!" A'na said, "OK, let us begin." We are going to set our intention to ground ourselves with Mother Earth first. Lucy, I want you to pretend that you have a long silver "connecting cord" that originates from the base of your body. Imagine if you will that you are sending that cord down into your Mother Earth to a depth of 40 feet and now you are going to set the hook, anchoring yourself to Mother Earth. At the same time imagine you are sending your energies of Love and Light down to Mother Earth and you are receiving her energies of Love and Light and you are now giving and receiving those energies as you imagine yourself becoming an infinity symbol, with no beginning and no end. Imagine this being so, and so it is. See this in your mind's eye.

'A'na, can I ask you why we are sending a pretend cord down into the earth?" asked Lucy. "I am glad you asked this question." replied A'na. Grounding is very important. There is an energetic cord that connects you to the Earth. It is an exercise that we do on Mentaka that connects us energetically to our planet. For you, this exercise allows you to ground yourself with Mother Earth. It allows you to be more authentically in your body, be in the present moment, and receive nourishing energy. Grounding allows you to use all of your talents and gifts, know their value in the world and give birth to your own visions and dreams. Grounding allows you to hold a safe, neutral space. When you are not grounded it is more difficult to create and achieve your goals and desires. You may feel unfocused and be easily distracted. You may feel anxious, or powerless. Do you ever feel like you can't concentrate, or that you feel spacy, or flighty? Have you ever felt like you are in quicksand? These are some of the ways you may feel if you are not grounded. Gravity may keep you on the earth and make you feel somewhat grounded but if you set your intent to ground yourself with Mother Earth, those feelings of shakiness will go away. When you are in your head, you are thinking more than feeling and in your body. You think about your feelings rather than feel them when this is the case. Some people may do this so they don't feel what is around them, energetically. These feelings would mean you are ungrounded Lucy. Your feelings are your guidance system and when you are in your head all the time you are ungrounded. I hope this explains what and why you need to ground yourself every day, several times per day.

In this meditation, I am going to ask you to imagine the scenario in your mind's eye as I describe our journey to you. Please feel free to make each scenario your own by adding the details you wish to my description. The more you make it your own the more you will receive from your guided meditation.

Ok, Lucy, we are beginning our little journey together. Please sit comfortably on our blanket, legs crossed and tucked into the body. If you feel uncomfortable doing so, you can sit another way. Lucy, I want you to take a big slow breath in through your nose to the count of four, hold it and let it go out through your mouth to the count of four. Good. Now, again, and three more times. Allow yourself to relax with each out-breath. If a thought comes in, just let it go by and return and focus on your breathing.

Lucy felt like she was about to board an airplane or cruise ship. She was so very excited to do this meditation with A'na by her side. She didn't know what to expect from herself. She told herself to just relax and listen to A'na's soothing voice and let it calm her and relax her. As she sat there, she was aware of the red birds call and the mockingbirds singing back and forth to each other. She heard the leaves moving back and forth like a whispering chime as the breeze came and went. She felt the breeze on her face, like a gentle kiss. She thought to herself that hearing the birds sing and feeling the breeze would be her background music. It was mesmerizing.

"Lucy, imagine we are walking out from our path in the woods into a big field of beautiful red flowers, see the flowers in your minds' eye, take their color into your awareness, into your body, breathe and relax. Imagine touching these red flowers as you reach out your hand," A'na said as she was leading Lucy into the sea of red with her angelic voice.

Lucy listened to every word A'na was saying. She saw the red flowers, red roses in her mind. She reached out to gently touch them as she walked through the field. She saw herself kneel down to take a better look at the roses. She even picked one of the roses and looked at it in her hand and then she heard A'na gently urging her onto the next field of flowers.

"Breath in. A'na said. Breathe out. We continue on and we are now walking into a field of orange flowers as far as the eye can see. It is a beautiful sea of orange. We stand in the middle of this orange sea, and we breathe in the color orange into our bodies. Look down at the orange flowers and see their beautiful color. Take one of the flowers in your hand. Together we are standing in the midst of the orange flowers, appreciating their beautiful rich color of orange. Breathe in. Breathe out. Relax," said A'na in her most gentle voice.

A'na's voice was so mesmerizing that Lucy felt like she was hypnotized. She was very relaxed and felt almost weightless. Lucy was trying to "feel" the color orange as A'na had suggested. We are continuing on our way through our next field of yellow flowers. We have yellow flowers on either side of our path. They are beautiful, waving back and forth from a gentle breeze. In Lucy's mind's eye, these were daffodils. Lucy loved daffodils. She could even smell their sweet fragrance as she walked by. "Breathe in Lucy. Breathe out. Relax. Relax and breathe in their beauty as we continue along the path. Breathe in their beautiful color of yellow." said A'na.

"On we go," said A'na in a most soft voice. "We are now walking into a field of tulips. The tulips are pink and green. We breathe in their colors as we continue to relax. Our spiritual hearts open wider as we feel the love in our spiritual hearts expand. "Breathe in. Breathe out. Relax," A'na said. "We continue on. As we walk along breathing gently, we lie down in the grass that is under our feet and we look up to see a big blue sky before our eyes. We gently and slowly take in the beauty of this big, expansive blue sky and continue our journey, relaxing even more. As we continue along our path before us appears a field of indigo flowers, a deep inky blue that feels our body with its pristine beauty." In Lucy's mind, she sees her grandmothers' Irises. She remembers them well. They are big and tall, almost coming above Lucy's knees in her mind. They are beautiful and sweet-smelling. She hears Ana's voice. "We breathe in this deep indigo color into our bodies. Breathe in . . . Breathe out . . . ," says A'na gently, and we continue on our path.

"We continue on our path, and we are now walking into a field of violet flowers, a most beautiful color of light purple. We look out as far as the eye can see to take in the beauty of the violet flowers. We breathe in this beautiful color of violet into our bodies," says A'na ever so quietly. Again, Lucy sees her grandmothers' irises. In her mind's eye, she bends down to smell their sweet fragrance. As she stands up, she is again aware of A'na's voice as she hears, "Breathe in . . . Breathe out . . . And now we begin to come back to where we started, and we open our eyes slowly." Lucy is aware of A'na's voice gently telling her to "Breathe in . . . Breathe out . . . Welcome back, Lucy."

Lucy opened her eyes half expecting to be on another planet. She felt like she was in a movie. It was like a dream while she was awake. She liked it. She was aware that she had a smile on her face. She looked at A'na warmly and knew she had to be an Angel of some kind. She wiped a tear from her face and thanked A'na for such an awesome experience. Lucy knew and became so keenly aware that there were forces bigger than she in control and she was thankful for A'na.

Lucy, we will call it a day for now. You need to get home and give yourself a chance to reflect on your thoughts and feelings about your first meditation. Drink plenty of fresh water. Relax and enjoy your evening with your family. You may want to write your thoughts down in your journal. "You can count on that, A'na." Lucy said, with an uplifted voice.

As Lucy walked home that afternoon, she found herself humming and skipping, looking at the birds, the trees, and all of nature as she reflected on what A'na had told her about everything having a consciousness. "We are all connected and communicating," she said aloud. She thought she would be up all night just writing in her journal and listening to her recorder. She knew in her heart that she was part of a miracle, a beautiful miracle. She knew no one would believe her story about A'na, or the spiritual truths A'na was sharing with her, but she knew it was true and that would be good enough for her at least for now.

Chapter 9

Our Source

It was the third day of meeting at the creek with Lucy, A'na decided to talk about creation. She did not know what beliefs Lucy had in her mind. She had decided she would tell her spiritual truths from her perspective on a 5th-dimensional planet. It would be up to Lucy to decide and discern what spiritual truths she would call her own someday. **A**'na was happy to share what she knew in her spiritual heart with Lucy.

Lucy had a good and deep sleep the previous night and again was ready to lear**n** more. This is the kind of stuff she wanted to learn. She headed towards the woods and noticed the blue jays again. They were close to the edge of the woods. She knew that they must have their nest nearby. She nodded to them and said: "Good Mornin**g**!" and then headed on her way to A'na. After a hello and a hug, sh**e** and A'na began their discussion. A'na told Lucy their planets, Mentaka and Earth, were two different learning environments. Lucy nodded and said, "I see." But before we go on with any further discussion about their differences, I want to talk about how they are the same. "Lucy," A'na said, "We are al**l** created by the "ONE," our Source. We are all a part of something much bigger than ourselves! All creation is created by the same SOURCE. I believe on your planet you have many names for our Source, but it does not matter what name we may call our Source, we are all created equal. On planet Earth, I believe many use the term, God or Allah. We are all divine, all eternal beings of light after we drop our vessel, our body. On our planet Mentaka, we are born into this knowing, and it is further nurtured and guided by our family and loved ones on the planet. The love and respect we have for each other and all of creation is reinforced by example. The whole planet and its inhabitants are in constant communication with one another. We are very aware that all are connected. It is a subtle communication. We are also in communication with our "Higher Self" on the other side of the "veil." Lucy had to interrupt A'na. "What is the veil?" asked Lucy. "The veil is the illusion of what we see before our eyes," A'na answered matter-of-factly. She went on to further explain this to Lucy. She said: "You see as I said we are all created equal, but while on the other side we are what we refer to as "streams of consciousness." While on the other side we are aware of everything, we share our knowing and understanding of life while in this stream. This is true for all souls, including you, Lucy. There are no secrets of any kind, nor are there any judgments of any kind. Like the drops of water in the ocean, that may seem separate, but all are the ocean."

I feel that I need to elaborate a bit more. While in human form on a 3rd-dimensional planet or 3-D reality program you tend to make everything singular in your mind when in truth it is not. It is a giant web of connectedness that is always occurring, always. I want to put some clarification in this for your knowledge. Because of your nature while in your physical reality, you, (and I mean most of the humans) on your planet tend to think in singular terms and then you project it onto everything that surrounds you, even when you think about or discuss your non- physicalness. The non- physical is anything but singular, being connected in all ways at all times whether you are consciously aware of it or not. The non-physical is a web of interconnecting possibilities, probabilities, dimensions, and "time periods." When we are non-physical beings, we possess many selves; past and present, probable selves and selves yet to be. We are but one facet of the soul while being in physical form.

Lucy, I am going to introduce a few of those terms to you so that you may have some clarity about them. The spirit is considered the nonphysical essence of you that you know of as yourself. It is the you with a physical body free of time and space. The spirit, like all other parts of your nonphysical self, is eternal. It is indestructible and free from the effects of what you may know while in human form, like sickness, aging, starvation, and more. The spirit is the closest you will come to your present physical individuality, once free of a physical body. Lucy, you must keep in mind that the spirit is one facet of the multidimensional person that you truly are. "Do you have any questions or remarks regarding what I have just shared with you, Lucy?" inquired A'na. Lucy was sitting cross-legged on the blanket, she had a blank look on her face. She was somewhere else it seemed, but all the while listening intently to A'na words. She thought about her grandfather's story. All of a sudden she burst out and said, "This is so cool. I am so lucky to have you sharing this knowledge with me, sharing with me and telling me things I may never have known. It is better than watching a mystery movie!" she exclaimed. (A'na laughed to herself.) With each truth A'na would share, Lucy would get chills up her spine as if she was affirming something she already knew but had somehow forgotten.

Are you ready to carry on? We going to discuss your higher self. Your higher self is your, for lack of a better word to describe it, your blueprint. It is the part of you that possesses all of your best and highest qualities. It is the part of you that you should always ascribe to become. It is the person that you can evolve into, from your present perspective. Lucy, you can always evolve into a better version of yourself. This self is a being that is both separate and part of you, always present and only a thought away. We can say that this being, your higher self, is what you will become, in the future, when you finish your evolvement. Your higher self is like a BFF (best friend forever!) This best friend has been with you in every lifetime and has all of the wisdom and knowledge from those lives, plus more. One can aspire to become their higher self.

Lucy was quiet and had a smile on her face. "So we are never alone?" asked Lucy. A'na responded, "You are only a thought away from any assistance. You may call our Archangel Michael, for example, if you are in a dire situation and need his help. You can call our for Mother Mary, or Jesus, or Quan Yin. These are just a few of the ascended masters. A'na, what are ascended masters? Lucy asked. I will give you a brief explanation, Lucy. "Ascended masters are the ones who have learned many great lessons from their physical lives and have transcended the life that they were living, seeing beyond what the eyes were seeing and going within for the answers they need." A'na answered.

"Are you ready to continue?" "I am," Lucy replied. We are continuing onward and upward. The next connection is that of your Soul. To your Soul, you are like a child, one of many! The Soul is an energy essence that takes many under its wing. When I said you are a facet, that is what I was referring to. It is like fingers on a hand. There are many selves to care for and nurture. The Soul is a nurturing force that directly shapes and molds the various forms of each of those aspects. It is your soul that helps you to become that higher self that you ascribe to be. You can call on your Soul when you are seeking guidance. Remember it is layer after layer, with each layer being of a higher vibration and all being connected.

The Monad is our next subject to discuss. It contains many Souls. The Monad is a direct aspect of the ONE. It is your Monad that is responsible for supplying you with your life force, our life force is what gives us life, our animation. When the spirit leaves the physical vessel, it is our life force that is leaving. The Monad is also responsible for the love and attention that you need to maintain your existence. It is probably hard to imagine all of these beings, energies, and layers that assist in our being, our Source has many helpers with many jobs. A life stream is a big JOB!

Lucy, I know that these are words and concepts that you have never heard in this life. I want you to know of the complexity, the magic, and wonder of creation. All of these selves exist and are, both part of and separate from you, me, all of us. It is like looking at a past reincarnate self. This past self is separate from you and yet it is a part of what you once were. All of these selves share the same kind of relationship. Because each of these selves is an aspect of you. There is a connection with each of yourselves. It is a connection that allows and enables knowledge to pass from a more evolved self to a less evolved self and what connects all the selves together. It is always to your advantage to maintain this connection between the more evolved aspects of yourself, this includes all that I have mentioned. "Lucy, I know I have given you a head full of thoughts and questions. There are those on your planet who know all of this and are sharing it with others." How about we get together tomorrow, and you can ask me anything you want about the other side," A'na said quietly. Lucy looked at A'na and shook her head in agreement. "I would like that," Lucy replied. Lucy gave A'na a big hug and headed towards home from the creek she had grown so fond of. She found herself in quiet reflection of all that A'na had just shared. It was all so amazing she thought to herself. She had to let it sink into her mind because she knew it was true, but somehow she felt like she had been deceived, lied to, or just not told the truth of matters before, but then she reminded herself that many did not know the TRUTH. Many were just passing down the information of what had been passed down to them without going any further or digging any deeper. They were caught in a cycle, she thought. She looked forward to hearing the rest of A'na spiritual truths.

Lucy arrived at the creek bright and early. She had a good sleep and was eager to know more. "Good morning, Lucy. I hope you slept well last night. Is there anything special you would like to ask me this morning?" inquired A'na. Lucy looked at A'na and asked, "Why do some people know and remember spiritual truths and others do not?" "Good question," A'na responded. Each of us is on our separate journeys. It is not about the destination but the journey itself. Many have been in life after life on your planet and maybe others not so many. I think it depends upon many things, such as the desire of the Soul and the evolvement of the Soul, and what lessons have been planned for and experienced for the Soul. I know it seems very complicated and it is in many ways. I think if you can silence your mind and listen to your spiritual heart you will find what it is you need. Love, forgiveness, and compassion for yourself and for others. "Lucy, I hope this helps to answer your question.

Lucy, for many they have gone from life, after life, after life without any awakening to their consciousness. This is where ascension comes into play. Ascension will allow (those who choose to do so) one to go into the stream of consciousness without having to replay life after life after life here on a 3rd-dimensional planet. This act of ascension will affect all of humanity in a positive way. Imagine if you did not have to view or participate in any of the things that you consider ugly, harmful, offensive, etc. ever again. Imagine. There are many ways of being, not just the human being.

Lucy was full of questions and wanted to wrap her head around the things that A'na was sharing with her. She asked A'na if she could change her reality? A'na responded with this answer: To change any "pictures" in your manifesting reality, you must simply shift the thought that holds the belief in place. Hmmm, Lucy thought, it sounds simple, but she knew it must be more difficult. A'na went on to explain it further. Lucy, as you spiritually evolve and the seeming separations (those thoughts that you have that you are separate from Source) fade away, the "Ring Pass Knot" extends, allowing the mind to accept more and more. This is often referred to as the "unfolding of your consciousness." A'na looked down to see that Lucy's mouth was open and she was just staring out into space again. "Are you OK, Lucy?" she inquired. Lucy looked at A'na and said, "You mean it is what I allow myself to believe in? What I allow to exist in my mind." Yes, yes, that is what I am saying. The ego and the psyche are powerful pieces of your being and will do many things to protect you from any perceived harm, even those of your own doing. Do not let this scare you. You must be vigilant in your pursuit of ever unfolding consciousness and the thoughts you allow and do not allow into your mind. Your ego and psyche will join on board as they see this is something that is beneficial for your being and not harmful to it. For example, you find a beautiful painting and believe it to be the most beautiful painting you have ever seen but it does not have your favorite color in it and therefore it is lacking. But let us say you if you could just appreciate the painting and not put any preferences or judgments on it other than to appreciate its beauty. That is what we call allowing. This brings me around to our next piece of the puzzle Lucy.

I would like to tell you a little about the veil of illusion. It is often referred to as the veil of illusion because you are in an illusory reality program. The mind is an amazing thing! I cannot explain the mechanics of how it all takes place, but I know there is much work that goes on behind the scenes, so to speak, (On the other side of the veil) before anyone takes on a physical vessel. There are many varied experiences one can have and have had.

We have had many in our past and future lives that we have come to love and care about. Think about that for a moment Lucy. You may have been the "mother one" to your "mother one" in another life. Your "mother one" may have been your son one, or your husband one or your daughter one in another life. This is reincarnation. What do you think about that, Lucy? "Well, I'm not sure. It seems kind of strange to think about

it that way." Lucy replied. "Fair enough," A'na declared. Let those thoughts set with you a while because this part is going to really get your attention. All of those other lives I mentioned you may have lived, are being lived right in this very moment. We say and refer to the present, the past, and the future but all we really have is this present moment. Time is a man-made illusion. It helps us to make sense and have a joined sense of coming together or meeting. It is a record keeper.

Our true home is on the other side of the veil. It is when we decide to take on a human form and go into the density of matter that we may forget some or all of this, especially on a third-dimensional planet like Earth. Everyone plays their part, from the evil father to the kind stranger. You are basically in a reality program. It is when you go within that you will begin to remember. You will become aware of being aware. You become the observer of yourself, your actions, and your reactions. While in our home on the other side of the veil we decide what situation and circumstances will make the lessons we desire to have come into our experience. Don't you know the angels have their hands full, making the arrangements for certain events, circumstances and people to all be at the right place at the right time for certain things to maybe be able to happen? It is all EXPERIENCE. I imagine it is a grand work of art and takes many helpers (Angels) who have many situations available to occur. It would take meeting or knowing the right people at the right place at the right time. Now that is an EVENT COORDINATOR! We keep the angels busy! That is what I mean when I say there are no accidents, no coincidences. There is an old saying that you may have heard. It is called a "God Wink." It refers to the Universe aligning all of the details to see that things can possibly happen a certain way.

Lucy and A'na were aware and both were feeling that they were part of a beautiful miracle in this very moment. It was something that neither one of them could deny.

There is so much meaning to our lives and the events that surround them, what you may call a miracle. It is often after an event or occurrence that we may realize a miracle has occurred. Your planet is keeping many angels employed, so to speak. Miracles happen every day! Lucy, it is all good! Even the bad. Please try to always remember this. It is your job to be happy, no one can do this for you, only you. The happier you are, the higher your vibration.

Lucy, I understand right now you see yourself as an individual, separate from our Source, but you are an extension of that Source. Remember, there is no separation. You are the Soul. You have a Higher Self that is also a part of you. The Higher Self is that part of you that has been with you since the beginning, through your many incarnations to Earth and to other planets. Your Higher Self is yet another layer or part of you that remains on the other side of the veil. "Lucy, you are the stuff that stars are made of. All of us are. Never, ever forget this." said A'na. We have such a grand Source who has forgotten nothing. Remember, everything is energy! You are fixed design, here in this human vessel, but there are also many other probabilities of you. I am talking about the past you, the present you, the future you, and all their probabilities of those definitions. Confusing isn't it. It is nothing to worry about. Like I said it is all good.

This is the poem that we teach our children early in life. It is called The Soul Mantra.

I am the SOUL
I am the LIGHT DIVINE
I am LOVE
I am WILL
I am FIXED DESIGN

It is a gentle reminder that we are each the SOUL, or a facet thereof. It also reminds us that as the Soul, you are also the Light of the One, the love, and the will. In physical form, you are fixed design. Lucy, there is never any need to fear your soul or that of spirit. You are always a divine being. Please do not ever doubt this, know it in your heart always. As you know this in your being you can share it with others. This is a good way to invoke/invite your Soul/Spirit to be present with you in all ways, in every moment. It is best if you say it aloud three times when saying the Soul Mantra. Take in a few big breaths through your nose and let the air out through your mouth. Lucy your Soul knows that this life is a gift! It is experience, many experiences. It is all good even when it does not feel that way.

Lucy, let's take a little rest as I know I have shared quite a bit of information with you. Lucy looked at A'na and said, "WOW, I am fine. This is great. Is our home on the other side what we call heaven? Is heaven up in the clouds?" A'na answered, "No not really, I think many do call our home on the other side of the veil, heaven. Lucy, many tend to believe heaven is up in the clouds but in truth, it is right here. You have to remember that everything is energy and that we, all of us are in different dimensions having different realities in our minds. Remember it is layer after layer that we are not seeing or are consciously aware of." "Lucy this is the REAL magic of life, just allow."

Lucy thought about her grandmother's and grandfather's, along with other family members and friends who had passed being in heaven, and how she would never see them again. That was the sad part for her, never seeing her loved ones again, thinking about never being with them. It was like they had just vanished and no longer existed, or that is what it had felt like to Lucy, as she shared her feelings with A'na, A'na had to intervene. "Lucy, death is part of the illusion of life on your planet. This is when we make our transition back into another way of being. We are all eternal beings of light. Lucy, love is eternal. You will see your loved ones again. For this present moment, keep their memories alive in your spiritual heart. Think about them. Love them and enjoy all of your good memories with them." With those words, Lucy took in a deep breath as chills came up her back. She felt like a weight had been lifted from her as she gave a sigh of relief. She explained to A'na that everyone she knew around her believed that death was the end and that we go up to heaven and rest in eternal peace. A'na responded: "I suppose if that is what you wanted to do, just rest, you could, but this is a huge Universe, there are lots of worlds to explore. There are lots of experiences to have." I don't believe you "rest" while on the other side. It is just another way of being. After you have transitioned and have a chance to "remember it all" things are very different in your mind and all is understood. Remember you will be greeted by angels, loved ones, and special beings to help acclimate you back home. You will be held in total unconditional love! This is a feeling we do not experience while in human form. It is much greater than the love we experience while in a vessel.

A'na decided that was probably enough information for Lucy today and asked if she would like to get in the creek for a while. She thought Lucy needed time to process all that had been said and shared today. They stood up and stretched, took off their shoes, and off they went to walk in the creek, happy, giggling, and smiling all the way. The two loved being together despite their age difference. A'na was a mature woman of what appeared around 30ish. She was more like 200ish. A'na was a flaxen-haired beauty with blue-green eyes and a beautiful dark olive complexion. She was quite tall and talked with the most precise wording. She had no accent. Her voice was soft and soothing and self-assured. She was thin, but not frail. Her beauty was striking. In contrast, Lucy was fair-skinned and red-headed. She had almost the same beautiful blue-green eyes as A'na. One could tell she was going to be a beauty herself. She was quite tall and lanky for a twelve-year-old girl. She spoke with a bit of a southern accent. Although she was normally timid around her peers and others, she was very comfortable talking to A'na. Lucy felt like she came "alive" when in A'na's presence. Lucy had an IQ of 150 and could already speak fluent Spanish and French. Her math skills were off of the chart and yet she was a very quiet, shy girl.

Lucy and A'na came back to sit on the blanket for a while, put their shoes on, and rested a bit before Lucy needed to head back to her home. She gave A'na a big hug and said, "I will see you in the morning." A'na continued to sit upon the blanket a while longer and pondered her day with Lucy. She was growing very fond of Lucy. She lay back on the blanket and looked up into the canopy of trees only to reflect on Mentaka and her family. The ones on Mentaka knew in their hearts just as A'na knew in her heart, there are no mistakes, and all would work out as it was supposed to. She gathered her things and headed back through the woods to her ship in the meadow, with the woodland creatures as her escorts.

A'na had taken her time walking back as she was enjoying interacting with her surroundings, the trees, the birds, the insects, and the woodland creatures. She had gotten back just in time to prepare for her sunset meditation. She spread the blanket onto the ground and removed her shoes. She grounded herself with the Earth. She took her time in imagining sending her silver connecting cord down into Mother Earth. She saw the cord going into Mother Earth's core and setting the hook, anchoring herself to this most beautiful energy. She saw herself sending her energies of love and light going into Mother Earth's core and the energies of Mother Earth coming up to her. She saw herself become the infinity symbol, giving and receiving those energies of love and light and it was so.

A'na lives in appreciation to the ONE. On Mentaka this is a way of life. To A'na all life is sacred, and nothing is taken for granted. She knows of the subtle life that is ever present before our eyes, even though we (most of us) have no idea. She can see and perceive what we call the invisible. She knows it to be a part of the intricate science and dedicated purpose of the ONE. To most of the humans on Earth, she may seem very strange with her perspectives of life being so much different than most of those on planet Earth. A'na understands that most on planet Earth are still very much asleep and are not aware of the mysteries and miracles of the unseen world.

She sat cross-legged on the blanket she had placed on the ground while facing the setting sun and noticing all of the beauty it offered in the evening sky. She felt the warmth of the evening sun on her skin. She set her intent to be grateful for her life, and all that it offered, including her surprise landing on another planet. She was especially thankful for meeting Lucy. She allowed herself to imagine walking into the beautiful aqua waters of the waterfall pool on Mentaka and floating on the water's surface. The colors began to swirl in her mind, and she was instantly transported to Mentaka in her mind. She could feel the water. She could smell the roses. She heard the waterfowl. She sat there motionless for almost an hour in gratitude. She arose to again wipe the tears from her eyes as she felt the love that was her source swell in her spiritual heart. She noted her feelings for Lucy with pause. A'na shrugged her shoulders for having any reservations about being lost. She gave in to the knowledge she had for Lucy being such a special young lady.

She sat and stared at the stars for a while. Noting several shooting stars going by. As she entered the ship, she said good night to the woodland creatures who had become her companions and guardians. She dictated the day's events into her recorder and then retired for the evening. She slept soundly that night and awoke refreshed the next morning. She had been taking a sponge bath each evening but was longing for a dip in the water somewhere. She would have to ask Lucy about a place to do so. She didn't think there would be such a place nearby, but oh, how she longed to submerge her body into a pool of water!

It was day four and the sun was about to rise. A'na laid out her blanket onto the ground and proceeded to do her sunrise meditation. She then prepared to meet Lucy for their continuation of spiritual truths. A'na packed a few things and headed into the woods toward the creek.

Lucy was departing her house just as A'na was heading out, they both arrived at the creek at the same time. Lucy had a big smile on her face and gave A'na a big hug! She said: "I am so glad you told me that I will see my family, my loved ones after they pass away. I miss my grandma so much. I loved her so." A'na looked at Lucy and said, "Love is eternal." She said no more and asked Lucy if she had anything she wanted to ask about yesterday's discussion. Lucy thought for a minute and asked A'na what are eternal beings of light? "Lucy," she said, "When we drop our vessels, our bodies, the spirit returns back to our home." It is believed that we are greeted by our family and many angels that will assist with our transition. It is also believed that there are beings of light on the other side of the veil that have remained there throughout eternity, never taking on a physical vessel. They remain on the other side working in the light, assisting humanity. On your planet Earth, you can make your transition at any time, but you are not consciously aware when it will happen, right? You can live to what you consider old age, or you can transition at a young age even before birth, correct? Lucy nods; "Yes." A'na tells Lucy, we call it transition because that is what is happening, we are making a transition in our being. Death is part of the illusion of life. To everything, there is a season. On Mentaka, we have the Cave of Rebirth, remember I had mentioned it earlier in our discussion? It is a sacred cave behind one of the waterfalls. On Mentaka after one has been in a body for at least 100 years, which is a very short time on our planet one can choose to go into the Cave of Rebirth. This is a sacred cave because this is where one goes after the decision to return home, to transition back into the stream of consciousness and take another journey or remain in the ethers. It is a sacred act and once that decision is made by an individual, it is respected by all on our planet. There are many hours spent alone in meditation before entering the cave for the purpose of rebirth. It is done by intent and deep meditation. Once one enters the "Cave of Rebirth for this purpose, it takes approximately 72 hours for the spirit to leave the body. After ninety-six hours the body is cremated, and the ashes are taken by the family members to do with what they may. On Mentaka we do not see our transition as sad because we know in our hearts that we will see each other again and again and again. However, we still miss our loved ones interacting with us in our physical lives and we may still have to grieve, but we move on with our lives, truly knowing we will see one another again. Lucy, here on your planet, it is much different, isn't it?

Lucy looked at A'na with big eyes and said, "Yes, it is very different." Lucy continued, "I have only been to five funerals, that is what we call it when someone has died. I mean to make their translation. "Lucy, you mean transition," replied A'na. Lucy continued, sometimes their body is in what looks like a metal bed, like a tanning bed, the casket is usually at a funeral home, or in a church. The person in the casket has makeup on and they are wearing their best clothes. They may be wearing fine jewelry. I have been told the jewelry is usually removed before burial.

Sometimes people choose to be cremated, rather than buried. There are many flowers around the persons' casket. People come and look in the casket and say goodbye to that person. They sign a register. Everyone is sad and crying. It is very quiet in the room near the body and in the other rooms. Later their body is taken in the casket and put into the ground in a cemetery or the body is removed and taken for cremation. Many flowers and wreaths are placed on the casket and nearby. A cement tombstone or a cement marker is usually placed where the person is buried. It has their name, their date of birth, and the date of their death. Sometimes there is a memorial for someone who has chosen cremation instead of burial. Again, everyone is sad and crying. I felt confused and sad at the funerals I attended. Nothing was explained to me about any of this. I just thought they were dead, gone forever. I felt like there was a hole in my heart when my grandma died. I was very sad, and I was crying. People would hug me and tell me how sorry they were for my loss. I thought I would never see my grandmother again. Many families who have had loved ones to die during the covid 19 epidemic have not been able to have funerals. It is very sad.

"Lucy, although it does feel like loss, it truly is not. You must allow yourself to grieve, to feel the loss or absence of the person who has transitioned. They are fine. It is the ones who are in the physical who are not, sometimes. I hope that these words may give some comfort when you have had a loved one to make their transition. Let your sadness turn to joy as you realize those who have passed before us still exist. Realize that they are present for us, wanting our happiness to surface. Know in your Heart that Love is truly ETERNAL. You will "see" one another again, I promise.

Lucy realized when she thought about death and losing her grandmother, the way that A'na had explained it made her think about it differently. She felt like a load had been lifted from her heart and it had caused many other thoughts to come up.

She realized it was how you choose to think about things that determine how you will feel about them. It was like a light bulb had been turned on in her thought process. She realized some of her friends who had loved ones to pass could not even talk about them or sometimes even say their name. Lucy made a decision that day that she would rejoice when she thought about the good times with her grandmother and the good times she had had with her. She decided it would bring a smile to her face to talk about her grandmother or to say her name. She would be alive in her spiritual heart, and she would love her forever, and with realizing this, she also realized that her grandmother loves her through eternity as well. Love is ETERNAL! Love lives in eternity. It brought chills up her spine and it brought a smile to her face and love to her heart.

Lucy, you know it is perfectly OK for you to be sad when a loved one makes their transition. It is different for each person. Grief is different for everyone. We all experience it differently. You must be patient with yourself and with others. Grief can shut down the spiritual heart. It is a very heavy energy that goes directly to the heart. "Lucy, I want you to know death, as you call it, is not the end. Death is merely a transition of one way of being into another way of being." A'na said in a soft voice as she gently placed her hand on Lucy's shoulder.

A'na told Lucy there is nothing wrong with feeling sad when you have a loved one to make their transition. You will miss your loved one or your friend. We too miss our loved ones when this choice is made. On Mentaka we look at the big picture of life, because we "know" and "remember" the big picture. If we are sad, it is ourselves that we are having these feelings for, our loved ones are perfectly fine. We are crying for ourselves and feeling our loved one's absence from our presence. Lucy, it is up to each individual to find and maintain our happiness and joy in life. On Mentaka, we see transition from the perspective of the soul. We know in our hearts that this is the choice of the soul, when our loved ones have chosen to transition from one way of being into another way of being. We will miss them being with us physically. After a transition on Mentaka, we have a large celebration with hundreds of candles being lit in their honor. We still talk about them. We say their name and we make references about the times we had together on the planet. We rejoice in the good times we had together. They are never forgotten. We keep their memories alive. It is like I told you. Love is eternal. You do not stop loving them nor do they stop loving you. Your loved ones are but a thought away.

A'na just reaffirmed what Lucy had figured out for herself. She realized that each soul has a separate journey. It does not matter the age we are when we pass. It is each souls' journey and experience. On planet Earth people talk about how the "good ones" die young or how their life was "too short" or how they had lived to "a ripe" old age, but it does not matter when you look at life through the eyes of the soul. Lucy was internalizing what A'na was sharing with her and her life would never be the same. She was changing the way that she had perceived life and the definitions she had placed on things having to be a certain way. She knew if she could just be open-minded, and allow, spirit would take care of the rest. She was finding internal peace at a very early age, what many had searched for their whole lives, joy and freedom. Somehow Lucy knew she had a mission to do in this life. She felt it in her gut.

Lucy, this is a story that we teach our children on Mentaka at an early age.

Nymphs and Mayflies

In the bottom of our little pond lives a group of water bugs or nymphs as they are called. They live a happy little life together in the water. For this reason, they could not understand why none of them ever came back home after going to the surface of the water.

After quite the discussion they got together and promised each other that the next one that left for the water's surface must promise to return and tell the others about what happened.

It was not long until one of the groups felt the urge to depart from the bottom, remembering full well his promise to the others. He found himself lying on the surface of the water. In the process of emerging from the water's surface, he went through a transformation. As he gazed upon himself, he saw that he was now a beautiful Mayfly with wings!

Remembering his promise to his friends, try as he may to enter the water, he could not. He flew round and round and back and forth, but he could not enter the water. He felt sad and bewildered for a moment and then he realized that even if his friends saw him, they would not recognize him. He decided he would just have to wait for them to come and join him.

He flew off into his beautiful new surroundings joyously looking forward to his next wondrous journey.

A'na, I think that your way of perceiving a person dying, I mean making their transition is beautiful. It is much easier for me to understand, and I feel much better knowing that we will see each other again, even though we may appear different. Please, tell me more about your beliefs and your planet. I want to know more. I want to know it all! So, Lucy, you see death is not permanent. The loved ones that pass are merely off to their next journey. As we allow ourselves to see that death is a transition, we are also able to know in our hearts that it is not permanent. I am not saying you will not be sad or that you will not miss your loved ones but knowing you will see them again, knowing this in your heart will allow you to have some comfort. You will be able to look at life through the eyes of ones' soul. You will see and understand the big picture. You are the ocean, thinking you are a drop of water in the ocean, while in your human vessel.

Lucy, remember that I said I would tell you more about our "Cave of Rebirth"? As I had mentioned, it is considered the most sacred place on our planet, and it is located in the region that I call my home. It is located high up on a knoll above the highest waterfall. One has to climb uphill, over many terraces, until you come to several stone steps which lead to the entrance of the cave. It is a beautiful trek. There are large boulders to either side of the steps which have vines and flowers growing upon it. Once there, the entrance is almost hidden from ones' sight. It has large bushes covering it. Our children learn of its existence when they are ten years of age. At that time each young person is granted a visit to go within the cave and view it with their own eyes. All of us may or will someday choose to go to the "Cave of Rebirth." The entrance is fairly narrow, one person can enter through its narrow passage at a time, but then it opens up so that probably 30 or 40 people could be within its walls. There are lanterns throughout the cave providing ambient light. The lanterns offer enough light that one can see the many crystals within the cave walls. It is most beautiful. The crystals look like tiny jewels as they glimmer and glisten as the light hits their surface. One feels most safe and secure within the cave. There is a huge stone, approximately 8 foot long by 3 foot wide that has been in place since long before my birth that is used for meditation. A thick blanket of moss covers the sides of this stone, and a blanket can be placed on the top for comfort while in meditation. The visits usually have twenty or more people who come in to see it firsthand. It is strictly voluntary and most all want to know more about the cave. It is a thing of beauty and awe on my planet. I often lead many of these such visits. On our planet when one wants to take their next journey in life, they can choose to make their transition by intent after they have reached the age of 100, as I had mentioned earlier. It is not a decision that is made overnight, and much meditation is required before making the decision to drop one's physical vessel.

Lucy had been listening with an open mind and had a question she needed to ask. "Is the decision to go into the "Cave of Rebirth" for this reason, to take their next journey, considered a suicide?" "That is a very good question, Lucy. Let me see if I can explain this a bit more." On Mentaka, remember, we are brought up in a different dimension than yours at present, our thoughts and beliefs are much different than yours, and that is what makes this different than what you refer to as suicide. We do not have what you refer to as suicide on Mentaka. In suicide, one is trying to escape, to feel better from a perceived belief and the feelings it has brought upon one. One is not in a good place mentally, not thinking clearly. A transition with intent is entirely different. There are many things that must happen before one can drop a physical vessel with the intent of doing so alone. It takes an adept, one who has gone into deep, deep, transformative meditation and is in touch with the God force within, one who has listened to their higher self without doubt and is ready for a higher service to others. It is not done to escape from anything, feeling, or belief. One knows in their spiritual heart that this is the next step in the evolution of their soul. Lucy, I hope this gives you a better explanation and answer to your question. It is the love of Source in service to others. One can always choose to stay in your physical vessel until your transition comes.

Lucy, right now much chaos and confusion are taking place on your planet. This is part of going from a 3rd dimensional to a 4th and 5th dimensional planet. People are very frightened, sad, and angry. There is much change and upheaval taking place. Many people are losing hope and are scared. Many have passed and many more will pass before this pandemic is over I think, but please, dearest Lucy, do not let this fright take hold of your thoughts. What I am sharing with you about my planet and our fifth-dimensional life is where your planet is headed, believe it or not. Your planet is on the cusp of change and with any change comes upheaval. Many things are being rearranged and other things are being brought to the surface. The dark way and doings of the past are being brought up, talked about, and looked at. A new way of thinking is taking place and with this, consciousness is being awakened. The people on your planet are beginning to be aware of their thoughts and actions. Some are beginning to take responsibility. The light and the dark are fighting this one out, but the light will win! It is that time in the history of your planet. You are in the cycle of time that is called the Age of Aquarius. Your planet is in the very beginning of making these changes. It will take time, much time. You just have to hold the light! Your light is so very important. Do not lose hope, ever.

"Lucy, I think I have given you some very deep and emotional information about the "Cave of Rebirth," maybe we should call it a day and allow you to take this into your being and ponder on it. How about we meet up in two days?" A'na felt that Lucy needed some time to herself to reflect on this information. For a young girl of twelve on planet Earth, in a third dimension, this was a lot to understand. She gave Lucy a big hug and sent her on her way. Lucy hugged A'na back, ever so tightly and told her she was glad that she had not gone into the "Cave of Rebirth" for her transition. A'na looked at her with a smile on her face.

Chapter 10

The Dimensions

The two days passed quickly, just like the days of spring. It was summer now and the days were getting noticeably hotter. "Lucy, are you ready for a new subject?" asked A'na. "I am," replied Lucy. "I am enjoying all that you have to share with me." She made herself comfortable upon the blanket that they shared as she placed the water and fruits to her side.

Lucy, I want to break this down and tell you more about the ones in physical form. Right now your planet is in the 3rd dimension, and the planet and her inhabitants, (those you choose to do so) are going into the 5th dimension. The dimensions have varied and specific definitions that go with them.

Lucy had taken very detailed notes and recorded everything that A'na had shared with her. Although she was just twelve years old, she found all of the information that A'na was sharing to be of the utmost importance. She wanted to be able to look back at her notes, listen to her recorder, and remember all the words that A'na was saying. She would be able to go over her handwritten notes and add anything she may have missed. Lucy was supposed to be in the tenth grade, having been promoted a grade above while in the fourth grade. She was not in school at this time because of the Covid-19 that was in its' fourth phase. People were still not sure what they were dealing with. Lucy was so intrigued with A'na's teachings she felt this was her school!

A'na began by explaining to Lucy what a dimension is. In physics and mathematics, the mathematical space (or object) is informally defined as the minimum number of coordinates needed to specify any point within it. Thus a line has a dimension of 1D. Because only one coordinate is needed to specify a point on it. A surface such as a plane of a cylinder or sphere has a dimension of two (2D) because two coordinates are needed to specify a point on it- for example, both a latitude and a longitude are required to locate a point on the surface of a sphere. The inside of a cube, a cylinder, or a sphere is three-dimensional (3D) because three coordinates are needed to locate a point within these spaces.

A'na went on to explain that in spiritual terms, there is dimension after dimension. Each dimension has properties that define it and realities that operate within it. The fourth dimension of the world is a four-dimensional space. The four dimensions of spacetime consist of events that are not absolutely defined spatially and temporally but rather are known relative to the motion of an observer. A'na went on to say that the state space of quantum mechanics is an infinite-dimensional function space. Each dimension has a higher vibration than the previous dimension. This is not to say that the higher the vibration the better. It is about the journey, not the destination. Remember that I am a fifth- dimensional humanoid and many on your planet cannot "see" me because of that. When those beings of a higher dimension come before us from the other side, they must lower their frequency and "we" must raise our frequency to have a "conversation."

Lucy, I will stop here with the mathematics of the dimensions as they do tend to get a bit more scientific. I just wanted you to know that our universe is not a random place but one of structure, structure created by the One, in the form of what we call quantum physics. I like to refer to it as Sacred Geometry. These shapes are communication. Here is a chart of the lower dimensions and the properties that define each dimension. As you see, Earth is currently a third-dimensional planet. Your Earth is in the process of going to the fourth and fifth dimensions and you can go with her if that is what you choose to do.

Lucy was not confused by the charts and their descriptions, but she was concerned by the way in which one makes the choice to join Mother Earth in the 5th dimension. Lucy asked A'na, "When do I make this choice and how do I make it?" Lucy was very concerned about it and wanted to know more. "Lucy," A'na replied; "You will know." "There will be no question if you are ready to make the leap to a fifth dimensional Earth." Your planet Earth is already preparing for this leap to the fifth dimension. That is why I am giving you and sharing with you as much information and spiritual truths as I can. You made this choice before coming into a physical body to be on the planet at this time. You and all the others, yes for many different reasons. You are not consciously remembering your decision at this moment, but you will know when the time is right for you. You will re-member.

A'nas' reassurance gave Lucy some comfort, but she still felt a bit perplexed. She was interested to look at the chart and see the properties of each dimension. As she came to the dimension for the rocks and minerals, she realized that they have a consciousness too! "A'na that is why you can feel their energy. Can I feel their energy too?" Lucy asked with enthusiasm. "Lucy, anyone can learn to feel energy!" A'na responded. Lucy was excited. She was going to bring in the crystals that her grandfather had found on their farm, but she would wait for the right time. Lucy, each crystal has a metaphysical property associated with it. There is much information about crystals. We will talk in greater detail about crystals in a bit. For now, I want to go on to our next subject.

During the next few days together, A'na continued to inform Lucy about many subjects and answer any questions that Lucy may have had. Lucy, I want to share as much information as I can with you. I think it will help you to assist others now in our present time and in the coming years. There is much I cannot teach you; you will have to do that on your own. For the present, we are "peeling the onion" and you are the onion. We are peeling back layer after layer of beliefs. Some will take up arms to defend their beliefs. This simply means they are not ready to move forward or to remember. Your patience and love will allow them to disarm themselves, mentally and some physically, and prepare for a new way of life, a better way for all. Many have been asleep for lifetime after lifetime, and this is OK for we are each on our separate journeys. It is not about the destination. But what you are learning, going to learn and remember will allow you to let go of preconceived boundaries and judgments. It will allow you do get past the imagined boundaries you place upon yourself. Our judgments and beliefs often hold people captive in their own personal prison. As you allow yourself the freedom to observe your life you open your own cage door and you are FREE.

Lucy, take these charts but don't try to remember everything at once, just familiarize yourself with them. You will have time to get to know all of this at some point. For now, just be open and allow. The most important thing I want you to do is to ground yourself every day and meditate each day. I will see you tomorrow, dear one.

Chapter 11

Loving Yourself

Lucy, this is a very, very important practice for you to incorporate into your daily life. There are many, many people on your planet that are stuck in thoughts of not being good enough. They may have thoughts of guilt, anger, jealousy, and other lower vibrational thoughts. I want you to always know that you, we, are the only one that judges ourselves. Any and all perceivable transgressions are forgiven when absolution has taken place. Absolution is as if it never happened. Our Source is pure unconditional love, and we are those extensions of Source energy. Always know this in your heart. Always know and remind yourself about the unconditional love from our Source.

This is something you can share easily with your family and friends. The practice of self-love. For many may feel uncomfortable about loving themselves because they think it is wrong or vain. You cannot truly love another without first loving yourself. This love is not romantic/narcissistic love, but divine love. The love that flows through us from our mother/father God. Romantic love can produce some very beautiful moments. Life is so good when you are falling in love, your step is lighter. You are happier and things don't seem to bother you. Your vibration is higher when falling in love. This love is just the tip of the iceberg compared to the divine love I am referring to. You are just getting a hint of what life can be when love is part of our lives. These are some of the steps that can allow divine love to be a part of your everyday existence.

To define self-love I would have to begin by saying it is the act of accepting yourself as you are, just the way you do for others you care about. Lucy, I would venture to say that most people on your planet at this time have not been taught to love themselves. On your planet it is considered to be selfish, which brings about feelings of being bad and thus lowers the vibration. I am not talking about actions which place you in a place to come in first or be seen as the best at something. What I am talking about is self-acceptance, love without conditions. Ego is in charge when we strive to do those things I just mentioned. What I am talking about comes from the spiritual heart. Sure most people can take care of themselves, bathing, wearing clean clothes, brushing their teeth, eating, etc. and although this is part of self-love it is not all of it. I want to expand your understanding of self-love. True self-love involves acceptance of ourselves with all of our perceived faults and shortcomings. Just like our fur babies love us without preconceived conditions and acceptance. Our fur babies are the perfect example. If everyone can love themselves as their fur babies do, we are halfway there. Your pets are teaching you about love without conditions. They have no preset conditions for loving you!

Self-love flows from our Source, it is a birthright. It is our most powerful, beautiful, heart-filling emotion that we can experience. We are experiencing just a small amount of this enormous love, as humans. As you allow this love to flow through you and become aware of it, you are automatically changing your life and your world for the better. You are raising your vibration! You are changing your world and helping to evolve it. This is the time for light and love to prevail on your planet. Lucy this is a glorious time for your planet and it is known all over the Universe. We are all waiting in glorious anticipation for your emancipation into the fifth dimension. You chose to be here now, although you do not remember it at the present moment. Lucy, as you become aware of and allow this beautiful love energy to flow through you, you will begin to see this love in all you meet, the people, the plants, the trees, the animals, and your planet. You will begin to see for yourself and understand that we are all connected. The Universe is a giant web of connectedness, just like the world wide web on the internet. You can become the observer of your own life and the circumstances that may befall you. You can be knocked down and bounce back without your thoughts and emotions controlling you. You will be able to respond instead of reacting.

Lucy, self-love encompasses the following:

Acceptance as you are.
Being gentle, kind, and patient with yourself.
Forgiving yourself.
Taking action based on your heart-centered voice within.
Self-care (mind, body, and spirit).
Healthy habits. (How you exercise, eat, and how you spend your time).
Holding a state of appreciation for yourself.
Accepting your weaknesses and your strengths.
Holding high regard for your own well-being.
Being able to say "no."
Respect for oneself and all of life. Being true to yourself.
Following your passion. What makes YOU happy in life.
Find your joy.

Lucy, this is probably the most important aspect of being your best self. When self-love is acknowledged and put into practice each day, we find our appreciation of and respect for our own worth and value. This very special love spreads into all of life. It begins when we can observe our actions with compassion as if we are our own best friend. We love ourselves without conditions. This will be difficult for many as they have been taught that loving yourself is a word your 3rd dimension has used freely, "selfish." The word alone brings a feeling of guilt and negativity with it. Lucy the truth of the matter is: if you can't love yourself, how can you love another? When you allow yourself the gift of self-love, life begins to change! Letting go may mean some big changes! Some changes may need to be made in your lives, and in yourselves to see, find and realize peace, joy, and happiness. When you practice self-love, you are going to take an honest look at yourself from the inside out. Where there is hate, let there be love. Lucy, I know this may seem harsh to you but there are many on the planet at this time and other times that are filled with hate. They are hurting, angry, sad and many have lost hope. Lucy, I really don't feel like you are capable of this emotion. You have not been exposed to hate, but I am sure you have witnessed it on television and in life. It is not a part of your being.

A good way to put self-love into your daily life is to sit in silence and set your intent to truly feel the divine love that is always there for you. The creator is within. The creator is without. Lucy, "Listen with your spiritual heart, not your brain. The spiritual heart only knows truth." Remember you are a spark of the Divine. Take a moment and feel this love coursing through your veins. Everything is imbued with the energy of Divine love. Take the time to recognize it, to honor it, and be it. When we set our intention and state our intentions to receive Divine love we give ourselves the best gift life has to offer. When we allow this love to be a part of ourselves, we begin to see it in everyone and everything. We begin to heal from the inside out. We feel alive and energetic. We know we belong. We know that we are a part of everything in existence. Remember you are the ocean, not just a drop in the ocean. It is this Divine Love that is the true catalyst for change and healing. Divine love is our birthright, and it is in every one of us for the asking.

Lucy was in awe of learning about self-love and the importance that it held. She was in deep thought about all that A'na had shared with her and had taught her. It made her feel so very special and yet she knew she was not. She understood that she had been given this opportunity to learn and awaken. She understood she was that drop of water in the ocean, but more than that she was the ocean too. It gave her great comfort to know and understand that there was something much greater than herself and that she was an extension of that, our Source. She knew she must share this knowledge and practice with others so that they too could awaken and remember just as she was doing. She knew she was part of a beautiful miracle and it sent chills down her spine. She had tears in her eyes. Lucy took in a big breath and let it out. She and A'na agreed to take a break over the next couple of days. A'na always thought it important to allow Lucy time to integrate her thoughts and reactions of the previous days. She had shared much with Lucy over a short period of time.

A'na was so enthralled in her work with Lucy that she would forget that she was stranded on another planet, but somehow it really didn't seem to matter. She knew in her heart that she was part of the change that was taking place on Earth and that Lucy would also be a huge part of helping others to understand and not be afraid of the changes that lie ahead. She wanted Lucy to know that it is all good, no matter the conclusion. She wanted her to know in her heart that it is all part of the illusion that we call life. A'na knew that Lucy and she had a mission of some kind, and it was being played out before her eyes. She reminded herself to get out of her own way and let the circumstances flow without attachment. There was one problem: she was growing so attached to Lucy. She was one so easy to love. She was an open book, kind and gentle. She would never forget their time together, no matter what as she also reminded herself, love is eternal.

Over the next day or so A'na updated her journal. She grounded herself with Mother Earth and went into deep meditations with the intent of seeking the counsel of her Higher Self. She allowed herself to be weightless and relax into "the knowing" that was a part of her being. She set the intent to send her love and light out into and throughout planet Earth. She imagined speaking with Mother Earth and assuring her that she was being assisted on many levels and her people were coming around to knowing that she is a living consciousness just as they are. Many were realizing this, and more were coming to her rescue. A'na realized that Mother Earth had been abused far too long with disrespect, and dishonor, with pesticides, and other poisons and chemicals. Her oceans were full of trash, her fields were overused, and her minerals were being used up. Her icecaps were melting as a result of gaseous emissions and pollutants. It saddened A'na but she knew in her heart that this was part of the learning scenario that had been created long ago. What happens here in the physical plane can seem like an eternity, but in eternity it is mere seconds. She finished her meditation with a prayer. The days had passed quickly since her last encounter with Lucy, but today they were to meet at the creek and resume class.

Lucy quickly dressed and did her chores around the house and farm. She was so much more aware of life that had always been teaming around her, the plants, the animals, the sky. It had taken on a new meaning for her, and she somehow felt more alive herself. She had a purpose in life. She knew she would help others with the knowledge that A'na was teaching her. It touched her heart on so many levels. She gathered her water and snacks for her and A'na to share and off she went down the now fully visible path to the creek. The path in the woods was beginning to look very used and worn. As she arrived all the gang was there to meet her, the woodland creatures and A'na. They gave each other a big embrace and all settled in. It was a bright sunny day, and the temperature was beginning to get a little warmer in the afternoons. Lighter clothing would be required and maybe a jacket for the early mornings. The tree canopy was fully mature, and the landscape had changed a bit. Lucy, are you ready to resume our talks and discussions? Lucy replied, "You bet I am. I am more than ready."

Chapter 12

Ascension

"Lucy, this next topic is something that I briefly touched on earlier, Ascension. It is something that you have probably not heard of, but it is something that is being offered to many on your planet and the Universe during your present time, if one wishes to bring it about. When one ascends with the intent of remaining on the other side, it is the act of not coming back to a third dimensional environment again and again as has been done for the past several thousand years. You are being given a chance to 'escape' this descent into 'forgetfulness' and move along in your soul's journey.

"In the past, the humans on your planet have been caught in a loop of sorts, returning again and again and again, and, for the most part, not remembering any of the soul's lessons from their sojourns. With each life that has been lived, there has been another chance to 'learn' from the circumstances one has found oneself in. With ascension, it is now possible to move along, having learned and 'Remembered' or awakened to your real truth. This is one of the reasons that your light is needed at this time on planet Earth. There are many who have been and are awakening. They are standing in their truth and assisting others to 'remember' as well. This is part of the time period that is coming about as we speak. It is all a part of the shift that began on December 12, 2012. In the blink of an eye, things will change. I know it does not feel that way while you are here in your human vessel, but from the other side, it is a much different perspective that is seen. Eternity changes our perspective a great deal, and what may seem like a lifetime is actually mere hours, possibly. I feel I would be neglecting a big part of your teachings if I did not mention ascension."

Lucy sat in silence yet again, as she was taking in all of what A'na had just said. She understood what A'na was telling her, but she still felt like the rug had been pulled out from under her feet as she struggled to understand how her world as she had believed was really so different. She somehow felt like she had been betrayed and lied to. She had to remind herself that many were still "asleep." They were just as she was, not knowing, not remembering. They were going along and playing their parts, just as Shakespeare had said. "All the world is a stage and all the men and women merely players." It all seems so real, so life and death, so important, yet it is all some may have.

"What does it take to seek this deeper understanding?" Lucy was asking herself. She felt so fortunate to have met her dear friend A'na, who was helping her to gain such a deeper and important understanding of life and of the ONE. She was feeling so much more significant than she ever had before. It was not that she was any better, or more important, or had a greater purpose, but it was the fact that she was part of something much grander than herself and it was real! It was a feeling that satisfied every wish to belong. She knew there were so many more that were having her same feelings before A'na had shared her spiritual truths.

Lucy was understanding that the Universe is a big place, and if we thought that we were the only human beings and life forms, we were just kidding ourselves. We are too important. We are too loved for all beings to "live this life" and that is it?

We go to heaven? She knew there had to be more, and it was A'na's spiritual truths that had set her mind free. The pieces of the puzzle were fitting together in a beautiful truth of life. She had opened her cage door and was setting herself free. It was a grand feeling! She was eager to learn more, to know more!

Chapter 13

The Chakras

We are going to be talking about the seven main chakras. It is one of my favorite subjects to discuss with the children. Lucy the chakras are your spiritual energy centers. They are located in your body. Remember everything is energy! Just because you can't see it doesn't mean you can't believe it. Can you see love? And yet it is real. You feel love in your body, with your emotions. The chakras are our personal energy centers, connecting our physical body with that of spirit. They are our direct route to our spiritual knowledge; therefore it is important that our energy centers, our chakras, be clear, and balanced. Just like climbing a ladder, we want to start at the first rung and go up the ladder, clearing as we go.

Our emotions reside physically in our bodies. On a subtle level, our bodies communicate with the energies around us. Certain energetic impulses relate directly to certain parts of our body.

Each chakra represents a spiritual life lesson or challenge to help us gain a more in-depth understanding of our personal power and our spiritual power. We learn how to overcome obstacles, let go of emotional blockages and walk the path toward spiritual consciousness. This is one of our greatest realizations.

Remember, you are divine all the time, no matter what you are doing or thinking. We are going to clear the field for you to have a better connection, letting go of any beliefs that may be holding you back and affecting the flow of energy in your body.

Lucy, remember the guided meditation we did a few days ago? I took you through the many fields of different colored flowers. This was a chakra clearing meditation. The colors we walked through in the fields are the colors of your chakras. All of the beautiful colors influence and affect the chakras.

For many people letting go of limiting beliefs is a giant first step, one in which you have done so easily. For adults, it may be a little more difficult or not. Most would like to think of themselves as open-minded but in reality, life in the third dimension has one in duality, thinking they are separate from Source, separate from one another, when in truth, we are never separate from our Source, and we are all connected. Limiting beliefs can be sneaky, hidden in plain sight, and sometimes deep within the psyche. "Lucy, are you familiar with the psyche?" asked A'na. This is where our thoughts come from, not our brain. Have you heard the term "to push someone's buttons?" When you push someone's buttons you have come into emotions that have a big response. These are triggers. Triggers point to some thought or belief, or emotion that has been challenged or unearthed. Your discernment will be required as to how to proceed. Acknowledgment is often all that is required. A'na looked at Lucy and said: **"ACKNOWLEDGEMENT**, it can be a very powerful action in the mind." With acknowledgement comes realization and with that comes truth for the individual, and with realization change can be initiated, understanding can be had, and feelings can be let go of. Some may need some help with this process and others may not. There are those on your planet who think they must confess or have witness before a person of the clergy to provide clarity and forgiveness. Lucy it is not necessary. Remember, our Source is within and without.

If we, you and all others can just remember and know this we can forgive ourselves and others. We can let go of that which no longer serves us and move on. Ego cannot live in the present moment. It lives in the past and the future, presenting worry and grief, the "what ifs." That is why our present moment is so precious, although know this. The ego can become your friend.

Our emotions reside in our physical bodies. As our bodies communicate with the subtle energies around us, we can either choose to let go of or hang onto the feelings of our emotions. When we hang onto our emotions, feelings, and beliefs, energetic impulses may settle into a certain part of our body and correlating chakra and cause it to be energetically weakened or blocked. The chakras are seen as major focal points in which energy flows up and down the entire physical body. The chakras govern our well-being and the well-being of the body's physical properties. For humans, this is emotionally and spiritually.

Let us take the emotion of sadness, such as bereavement. Its feelings can have a long-term impact on our bodies because of the reasons for these feelings. You tend to think about the negative feelings associated with this sadness over and over. Hatred and guilt are other negative feelings that can last for long periods of time whereas fear usually passes quickly, and anxiety lasts much longer. We would consider these feelings to be negative rather than positive, closing down our energy centers rather than lifting, and opening our chakras, like feelings of happiness, contentedness, and love.

Getting back to our chakras. The more open and aligned our chakras, the more easily we are connected with spirit. Source is the energy that imbues everything, every blade of grass, every drop of rain, every molecule that we breathe, every cell in our bodies. We are better connected with Source when our chakras are functioning fully. A'na, I have a question. "I didn't even know there were things called chakras, does that mean I am completely blocked?" "Oh no, Dear one, it does not mean that at all." You will feel more alive, open, and energetic when your chakras are open with intent, but if you are aware and listening to your body and emotions you are open too. Remember your body is a consciousness too. You may not have known the name or location of these energy centers but another part of you is aware, very aware, and communicating with one another. Your body is a living consciousness too, with each organ, cell, atom and electron aware of each other. "What do you think about that, Lucy?" inquired A'na. "I think it is absolutely amazing! exclaimed Lucy. "Everything about all of the Universe is amazing! I feel like I have lived in darkness without being aware of so many wonderful things. I feel like the blind man who has gained his sight for the first time. I feel awed," replied Lucy.

Lucy, you are already more aware than you know you just have not put a label or words to this knowing. For example, feeling energy. When you walk into a room and there has been an argument. You feel this energy. You know that something was up. You were just not aware of what you were doing. Now you can acknowledge your awareness and your knowing, becoming more and more aware each day. Remember everything is made up of energy! A'na smiled at Lucy.

Back to the chakras. The chakras are the interface that allows us to be connected with spirit. We want to have our chakras, our energy centers, be open, clear, and vibrating in a clockwise motion for our optimum physical health and our connection to spirit.

Lucy, I am now going to take you into the knowledge and description of our seven main energy centers, the chakras as associated with the physical body. In truth, there is chakra after chakra, just like dimensions over penetrated going up the ladder. There are many, many more energy centers within the body, and there are chakras that go above and beyond the physical body, but we are going to concentrate on our main seven energy centers for now.

Our chakras are often called portals, or openings. This is where the soul makes the connection with the physical body to experience physical life. * It is said that the chakras are like transformers that transform energy between the physical and the nonphysical. Balance for the mind, body, and soul is our goal, Lucy. Each chakra is a holding place for certain beliefs that allow us to function fully, or we feel the effects in our lives and in our bodies. Life may become difficult. These beliefs can be misperceptions that we have taken on as our own, without truly thinking about them or even being aware of them. When this happens our chakras may slow or close down. This is when the energy gets stuck in our bodies and our lives Our bodies may reflect aches and pains from holding these misbeliefs. When we lose our connections with the nonphysical, we may feel powerless and limited in life. Lucy, I hope you find this as fascinating as I do. On Mentaka we have long ago navigated the seven main energy centers and operate on our knowledge and connectedness with Source as well as the other superimposed chakras within and without our bodies. It is a way of life for us. This is where your planet is headed if you wish to go with her. At this time much has been forgotten, but all is changing, and many will begin to remember, the body also remembers. It is called cellular memory. You have no doubt been on many planets and had many different physical situations. I know I am sharing and telling you much, things you may never have imagined, but if you can imagine it so, it can be so. Our Source, our Mother/Father God is the force behind our animation, our experiences and we must never ever forget that this life is a gift for us to experience many, many life situations, the chakras are a very important part of this. "Lucy, I feel like I have placed you in advanced training," said A'na. Lucy looked at A'na with a twinkle in her eye. She liked it. She LOVED it. She was soaking it all in. Lucy kept telling herself she was a part of a beautiful miracle. A'na knew Lucy to be an old soul and she also was aware Lucy already knew all that she was presenting to her and sharing with her. She was just assisting her memory to awaken and remember. A'na knew Lucy was/is a very beautiful soul with a very bright light. She was a pleasure to be around. Her innocence and energy felt so very comforting to A'na.

Lucy, please check your recorder as the chakra information is very detailed. Each chakra has one or more functions associated with it. I am going to give you a flowchart to look at and review. *

I will be including the Sanskrit word for each chakra. Lucy, Sanskrit is the sacred language of Hinduism. It is approximately 4000 to 6000 years old on your planet. Sanskrit means "refined," "consecrated," and "sanctified." It is the language of classical Hindu philosophy and of the historical texts of Buddhism and Jainism. It is considered to be the "mother of all languages on earth. It is regarded as the "high" language and used mainly as a ceremonial language for hymns and mantras. The Sanskrit word for chakra is "wheel."

The Root Chakra

The first chakra is called the root chakra. It is considered the root of our being. The Sanskrit word for the root chakra is Muladhara. "Root of existence." (Mula means "root" and dhara means "flux." It is symbolized by a lotus with four petals. It is the chakra that establishes the deepest connections with our physical environment and with the Earth. The root chakra is associated with your feelings of safety and security, both physical and metaphorical. This will include your needs such as food, water, and shelter, as well as your emotional needs. The root chakra is what causes your survival instincts, also known as fight or flight responses. It is associated with the color red and is considered to be divine masculine energy. It does not matter your physical gender, we are all meant to be balanced energetically in both divine masculine and the divine feminine.

The root chakra is located at the base of the spine, the pelvic floor, and the first three vertebrae. It faces downward toward the ground. It allows you to let go of fear. The root chakra is associated with the Adrenal cortex glands. It is your center for physical energy, grounding, and self-preservation. As divine masculine energy, it is courageous, fearless, and loyal. It aids in resilience and allows you to focus and use your organizational skills. It also aids in setting healthy boundaries for yourself. Your feelings of safety you may have felt as a small child plays an important role, safe or not. The root chakra is responsible for your sense of safety and security while on your earthly journey. This chakra is the first of the chakras of matter, (matter vs spirit). Through this chakra, you build a solid foundation for your bodily vessel. Your instincts are associated with this chakra. The Earth element is associated with your root chakra allowing you to dig in and feel firmly rooted. The energy of the root chakra is what allows you to harness your courage and resourcefulness with the will to live during times of great stress.

Lucy, now you know why this is the first rung of the ladder. The root chakra sets the foundation for you. As you know the root chakra is being challenged with the pandemic and other stressors on your planet. If there is an imbalance in the root chakra or it is out of alignment you may experience anxiety disorders, depression, or have fears and nightmares. There may be a change in weight gain or weight loss. A physical imbalance may manifest as problems in your colon, with elimination, or with lower back pain or problems, the bladder, legs, or feet issues. You may experience pelvic floor pain and/or incontinence. Prostate problems for men. Sometimes eating disorders may also be a sign of a root chakra imbalance. When the root chakra is balanced, clear, and open, you are open to abundance and trust that life's basic needs will be provided.

From an emotional perspective when out of alignment, you may bounce from one thing to another without focus or intention.

You may appear flighty to others. This may lead to exhaustion, anxiety, and stress. Feelings of lethargy, an inability to take action, and a feeling of being stuck. Everything may seem like a risk.

Grounding, remember we talked about grounding earlier? Grounding is an exercise that connects you energetically to the earth. It allows you to be more authentically in your body, and to receive Mother Earth's healing energy. When you ground yourself, you are taking in and soaking up negatively charged electrons, creating balance and healing. Remember, you can imagine sending your silver connecting cord from the base of your spine, down into Mother Earth to a depth of forty feet and set the hook to anchor yourself. Imagine giving Mother Earth your energies of love and light and receiving her energies of love and light and then imagine becoming the infinity symbol, giving and receiving those energies of love and light. Imagine it being so and so it is!

There are many and various exercises to ground yourself with Mother Earth. Walking barefoot and connecting, walking out in nature, and spending time in nature. You can also imagine yourself having roots like a tree and sending them down into the earth's core.

Since this is the root chakra, any earth color, and the color red will positively affect the first chakra. Oil of bergamot and sage will aid in opening and balancing this chakra. Sound at 432hz is another aid for the root chakra. Also, the sound of thunder. A didgeridoo or a deep baseline is yet another way to open the root chakra. You can also eat root veggies such as potatoes, yam, onions, and carrots to aid in opening your root chakra.

Mantras for opening the Root Chakra

I am deeply rooted.
I am supported by the earth.
I am one with my physical body.
I am safe and secure.
I trust myself.

Lucy sat there in silence with her mouth half-open. "Lucy, are you alright?' asked A'na. Lucy looked at A'na and asked her, "How do you know all of this information?" "This is the first chakra, only?" "Oh dear one, am I giving you too much information?" asked A'na. "No, no it is not that. I am just amazed at your knowledge." Lucy replied. A'na was quick to remind Lucy that she is a historian, and the Earth's history was one of her favorite subjects, including the humans of earth. A'na found the chakras to be fascinating, for all in a vessel, two legged or four legged. "Your Mother Earth is a very honored and respected planet among all in the Universe. Can you even imagine what a big beautiful, kind, and generous consciousness she is?" asked A'na. She is revered by the galaxy and many, many are in support of her in her endeavor to move into the fifth dimension. It has been long-awaited. She is greatly loved.

"Oh A'na, I am sorry. I did not realize this. I feel so ignorant." replied Lucy, almost in tears. "Do not cry, Lucy. You have been a great steward for Mother Earth and will do even more great things in your lifetime to rally behind her and propel her forward. You will be there with her in the fifth dimension! I know you will." declared A'na.

A'na was not sure why she blurted this out, but there it is, she said it. It had come through if she meant to say it or not. She hoped she had not scared Lucy with this information. She didn't want to put too much weight on Lucy's young shoulders at this time, although she knew in her heart that Lucy had a great mission and she was there to encourage her and give her the air beneath her wings to SOAR, to fly higher than she ever thought she could. She wanted only the best for Lucy in all ways and knew that she could assist many.

The Sacral Chakra

The second chakra is called the sacral chakra. The Sanskrit word for the sacral chakra is Svadhisthana, meaning, "where your being is established." "Sva" means "self" and adhisthana" means "established." It is symbolized by an orange lotus flower with six flower petals. At its center, we find two concentric circles that together form a crescent moon shape. The circles with it represent the cyclical nature of birth, death, and rebirth. The sacral chakra governs the reproductive system. It is represented by the color orange. Orange is the color of activity and aliveness. It is the color of purity, rather purified energy in the Hindu tradition, and monks and ascetics usually wear this color. The six petals symbolize the qualities that one is to overcome to purify this chakra. These qualities are anger, hatred, jealousy, cruelty, desire, and pride. It is located approximately two inches below our belly button. It encompasses the space between the belly button and the pubic bone and expands into the ovaries for women and the testicles for men. It is associated with the lymphatic system. This chakra governs your emotions, your creativity, your sensitivity, sexuality, your reproductive organs, intimacy emotional well-being, and self-expression. It is often referred to as the center of your pleasure and passion, both sensually and creatively. This can manifest as finding something we like to create as in music, art, cooking, or having fun, but on the flip side, it is about your sensuality and embracing your human sexuality. It is considered divine feminine energy and is associated with the element of water. Thus this energy is associated with our flow, flexibility, and emotions.

A blocked sacral chakra will express in sexual performance and lower back or pelvis issues. There may be issues with reproduction and urinary issues, addiction to food, especially unhealthy food. There may be an inability to express feelings, a lack of creativity, low self-esteem, and a desire to hide from the world.

The sacral chakra governs taste. Foods that may aid in opening this chakra are carrots, peaches, and or nectarines. Wear the color orange. Crystals that are considered supportive stones for the sacral chakra are carnelian, citrine, topaz, snowflake obsidian, moonstone, and more. Stones with orange, golden, or red-orange colors are considered helpful in supporting the sacral chakra, Keep the stones in your aura for approximately 8 to 10 hours or by your bedside table while you sleep, or in your pocket. You can also wear these stones as jewelry.

Mantras for the sacral chakra:

I attract people who treat me with respect.
I enjoy pleasure in all areas of my life.
My emotions are free-flowing and balanced.
I am a creative being.
It is my birthright to receive pleasure.'
I honor the sacred body in which my soul resides.
I welcome sensuality into my life.
My intuitive senses are awakened.
I embrace my vibrant sexuality.
Creating nourishes my soul and brings me joy.
I am a loveable and desirable being.
I am comfortable with my body and treat it with care.
I let go of past feelings that no longer serve me.
I breathe in powerful golden-orange light.

"Lucy, do you have any questions or comments about the sacral chakra?" asked A'na. "Would you like for me to slow down?" She inquired. Maybe we should just take a short break and stretch a bit. The day was young, and the sounds of nature abounded. The air smelled fresh as the scent of flowers wafted by. As A'na and Lucy looked around all of their nature friends were nearby. Lucy thought it was so cool to see them so close, just like human friends. She always loved nature and animals, so she was very comfortable having the woodland creatures nearby. It warmed her heart. Having A'na as a friend and teacher was also very comforting. Lucy felt so fortunate to be there with her and be a part of this learning scenario. "Are we ready to resume?" asked A'na. "Yes," replied Lucy.

The Solar Plexus

The solar plexus is our third chakra. The color associated with the solar plexus is yellow and it is located about two inches above your belly button. The solar plexus chakra governs the digestive system. This includes the stomach, the large and small intestines, liver, pancreas, and gallbladder. The symbol for this chakra is a yellow triangle that faces downwards, within a ten petaled lotus. It is the core of your personality. It is your personal identity and the center of your personal power. The Sanskrit name for our solar plexus is Manipura, meaning "lustrous gem." It is what gives you the courage to assert your willpower, pursue your dreams and pursue the things that may scare you. It provides the source for your warrior energy, relates to self-esteem and the power of transformation. When the solar plexus chakra is open it acts as a filter that keeps you from absorbing negative energy. It is the core of your personality and identity and the center of your personal power. When the solar plexus is open you have the courage to face your fears and the challenges of life. You can assert your willpower to do the things in life that may scare you.

The solar plexus is represented by the color yellow. When healthy it is a shining gem that enables you to "shine forth" in your wisdom and truth. The solar plexus is aligned with the element of fire.

Lucy was taking in all of the information that A'na was telling her, and she had come to the conclusion that she had blocks in the first three chakras. She would ask A'na to assist her with clearing them. She wondered if she had come into her vessel with these blocks or had they been brought about by her thinking and beliefs about herself? Lucy knew A'na could assist her in clearing up these energy centers.

The solar plexus responds well to aromatherapy. The essential oils of chamomile, bergamot, cedarwood, and rosemary. One can wear these aromas as well. Citrine, tiger's eye, yellow tourmaline, and peridot are the crystals associated with the solar plexus.

A frequency of 362hz will align and open the solar plexus. In addition, you can use the following mantras associated with the solar plexus. Close your eyes and envision or imagine a yellow ball glowing within your core and say one or all of the following.

I honor myself. I accept myself.
I am proud of my achievements. I am worthy.
I feel my power.

Lucy stopped A'na for a moment before she went to the next chakra. "A'na I have a question to ask," she said. "Do you have the same chakras in your body that we have in our body here on earth?" "That is a very good question for you to ask, Lucy. We do have the same chakras, but once all chakras are mastered and understood, other chakras are there superimposed upon the latter, meaning that other lessons are available for us to experience. The unseen world is vast and there are many chakras outside of the body, above it, and below it. I will not be discussing them at this time, but this is where your body will be heading with the "new" earth." Lucy seemed astonished by A'na's answer. She understood what A'na was saying but was in awe, just the same. She knew that A'na was like her own self in so many ways but yet so different in so many ways.

The Heart Chakra

The fourth chakra is called your heart chakra. It is located in the center of the chest. It is not the organ referred to as your heart. The heart chakra governs the circulatory system and includes the heart, the lungs, shoulders, and upper back. It is often referred to as the spiritual heart. The color associated with the heart chakra is green but can be seen as pink when open, to those who can distinguish such. The element it is associated with is air. The heart chakra is divine feminine energy and is represented by a six-pointed star within a twelve-petal flower.

The heart chakra is the center for our ability to unconditionally give and receive love. It is the energy responsible when you are unstuck, unhurt, and unbeaten as well as the ability to show compassion, love, and appreciation of beauty. As the center for connecting the lower three chakras: (the root chakra, the sacral, and the solar plexus), with the upper three chakras, (the throat, the third eye, and the crown). The heart chakra acts as a bridge between the earth and spirit.

Again, Lucy felt the chills go up her back as A'na was explaining the heart chakras role as a bridge between the Mother Earth and spirit. She found it fascinating. She was learning things that made so much sense to her and she couldn't understand why. Did she really know these things from another life she wondered?

Lucy is here at the heart chakra, that transformation and integration come together. The heart chakra when aligned, allows you to recognize you are part of something greater. You are able to understand that you are interconnected with an intricate web, extending through life on earth and the universe. When the heart chakra is open, and the energy is flowing freely you are loving to yourself and to others. Deep bonds are formed and recognized with other beings.

Lucy's heart felt like it just melted, as tears of joy ran down her cheeks. The heart chakra and its defined qualities had sent feelings of understanding and acceptance throughout Lucy's body and she truly understood what A'na was saying. Lucy felt humbled as she reflected on A'nas' description of the heart chakra and the beauty of its' being.

When the heart chakra has a blockage or is not in alignment we may have issues with the upper back, the shoulders, arms, wrists, respiratory and circulatory system. There may be issues with high blood pressure, insomnia, difficulty in breathing, and heart attack. You may have lung disease or heart disease.

As Lucy heard the description of the heart chakra, she immediately understood that there was not any disease on Mentaka. She asked A'na if she was correct in her assumption. "Yes, dear one, you are correct. We do not have illness or disease on our planet. It was long ago that it became something of the past." she replied. Lucy smiled and felt proud of herself for "seeing and understanding" this.

Emotionally, one may hold grudges, have trust issues, and fear of abandonment. One may be codependent on another and have difficulty expressing your emotions. One may show excessive isolation tendencies. Feeling lonely, being socially anxious or shy, being self-critical and judgmental of others, lacking trust in others, and being fearful of relationships are symptoms when your heart chakra is out of balance or blocked.

To open and align the heart chakra breath work that allows one to experience the sensation of the breath entering and leaving the body is a good exercise to do. The crystals, aventurine, rose quartz, and jade, either worn as jewelry, in the pocket or on the nightstand will assist in removing any blockages. 341.3hz is the frequency the heart chakra responds to, the essential oils of bergamot, geranium, jasmine, lavender, cypress, or rose are great oils in opening the heart chakra. Rose is the highest vibration flower essence. Breath in through the nose on the count of four and out through the mouth on the count of four. Breathe.

"Roses," Lucy whispered to herself. "Highest vibration flower essence," she repeated aloud. Lucy was internalizing A'nas' preference and love of the rose in another way. It was not just for the beauty of the rose, but for many reasons. It now made sense to her on another level.

The mantras associated with the heart chakra are

I forgive myself and others.
I am open to giving and receiving love.
I am worthy of the purest love.
I live with gratitude and generosity.
I live in harmony with all other beings
I honor the guidance of my spiritual heart.
I release and let go of all resentment.

I forgive myself for my mistakes and I grow from them.

Lucy, you are young and are getting a lot of knowledge from the spiritual truths I am sharing with you, but for many on your planet, living in duality has caused a feeling of separation, separateness from our Source (God) in many of your people's eyes and hearts. It is these beliefs that may be causing feelings of unworthiness, guilt and many of the feelings associated with a blocked heart chakra. I am sharing this with you so that you may be aware of this and give them the tools they will need to bridge this gap and misbelief about themselves. Remember, it was once that way on our planet long ago. Your planet has not always lived in darkness. There have been times of great light and knowledge. Shall we continue?

The Throat Chakra

The fifth chakra is your throat chakra. It is located at the center of the neck, the throat area of the body, and is the center of expression and speech. Biologically it is associated with hearing (the ears), the mouth, the neck, and the endocrine system, specifically, the thyroid. The color associated with the throat chakra is sky blue. The throat chakra relates to speaking "your truth." The throat chakra is about speaking and living the soul's truth, to carry out the divine plan for this life.

The Sanskrit word is Vishudda which means, center for, "especially pure." Or "purification." Energy becomes transformed into our manifestation in the physical world. Depending upon how clear or muddied this chakra is will determine our failures or our successes in life. It is important to speak our internal truth, that of spirit and the still small voice within. It is the passage of energy between the lower body and the head.

Your words contain power and energy. Your words should be said and used with intention and deliberate action for clear communication. This means taking your time and formulating your words correctly before speaking aloud.

Lucy, feelings of guilt will easily muddy or clog the throat chakra. I wanted to call this to your attention because humans, especially humans on a 3D planet are going to have guilt issues because of the "beliefs" that have been instilled into your belief system. It is often carried around like a ten-pound suitcase, letting it weigh people down. Some may feel guilty over things that they have accidentally said or did that may have been taken out of context. Some things may have been said in anger that one did not mean. Maybe you didn't go to church last Sunday or the last Sunday or never. It really comes back to what people play in their brains. This is where you will be able to help people to let it all go and start a new life this very second without any guilt. Send the guilt packing. Let it go! Think a better thought. It is experience. It is only you that is judging yourself, others, and outcomes, our Source is not judging. Unconditional love has no boundaries. Remember this always, Lucy. You can help others to know this in their spiritual heart.

When in balance one can offer sound advice when asked. You are creative and helpful. You know what you want in life and are not afraid to ask. When out of balance one may experience neck pain, thyroid issues, hormone fluctuation, sore throat, fever blisters, and/or TMJ.

When the throat chakra is overactive you are gossipy, opinionated, critical of others, and verbally abusive. You may yell. When underactive you may have an inability to express yourself, often being misunderstood or misinterpreted by others. You may appear wishy-washy, flaky or unreal. You have difficulty being honest with yourself and give mixed messages. Generally speaking, nothing will work out in life exactly as you like it to be.

The element of the throat chakra is ether(space) that forms the essence of emptiness. Our true selves exist in this space between the clutter of constant thoughts and emotions. In the calmness of silencing the mind through meditation, we can find the very subtle element of ether. The throat chakra acts as a bridge between the heart and the mind. When cleared, we can integrate the wisdom our soul has to offer.

So, Lucy, you can see that the chakras have so much to offer in terms of your spiritual growth and the advancement of your soul? "What do you think about the chakras from your perspective?" "A'na, I think that everything you are sharing with me is so beautiful. It makes me want to cry and it touches MY spiritual heart. I love the spiritual attributes of the throat chakra especially." explained Lucy.

You can clear the throat chakra with sound therapy such as singing, singing in your automobile, singing in your shower, and singing with a group, as in your choir. Use your voice, scream, laugh, groan, pick up a musical instrument. Play music that moves you.

Mantras for the throat chakra:

It is now safe for me to express my feelings.
What I have to say is worthy of being listened to.
I listen to and acknowledge the needs and wants of others.
I am comfortable in silence.
My voice is heard.
I am able to speak my truth with ease.
I am able to clearly state my needs.
I always speak from my heart.

My voice is becoming stronger and more compelling each day.

The crystals lapis lazuli, blue calcite, turquoise, blue tourmaline, blue agate, and celestite can be used or worn to positively affect the throat chakra. The essential oils of rose, frankincense, sandalwood, and jasmine all have a positive effect on our throat chakra. 384 hertz is the sound range for the throat chakra. Singing in the car, shower or choir are all great ways to balance the throat chakra.

The Third Eye Chakra

The third eye chakra or Brow chakra is our sixth main chakra. The Sanskrit name for the sixth chakra is Anja, which means "perceive." "Command," or "beyond wisdom." It is associated with the color indigo and is located between the brow lines. It is connected to the brain, the pituitary, and the pineal glands, as well as the skull, eyes, nervous system, and senses. It is often referred to as the mind chakra. The third eye governs the endocrine system. It also governs our perception, intuition, and insight and helps us to perceive both the physical and subtle.

The third eye chakra is the center of psychic power, spirit energies, and light. The third eye chakra sees everything as it is, from the point of "witness" or "observer" or simply being mindful moment by moment. When it is open, we not only see but we understand.

The third eye chakra interacts with the rational mind in order to deepen our intuitive insight to see beyond the veil of illusion. The challenges of the sixth chakra are opening the mind and discriminating between thoughts motivated by fear, strength, and illusion. It is learning to develop an impersonal mind and detaching oneself from the physical and mental illusions. When open we can learn to transcend our thoughts, our worries, and our fears and learn to truly know our souls from within. The third eye chakra holds a unique combination of fear, facts. personal experiences and memories that are constantly active within the mental body. Again, when fully open the third eye chakra gives us wisdom beyond our self-inflicted realms of "reality" or "realistic illusion." Ultimately, nothing is holding us back but ourselves. Only the mind has power over you and if we can control the mind, we can overcome any limitations we currently have.

"Lucy, I want to stop here for a moment because I have just said some very, very deep statements about our mind. What do you think about the description of the third eye chakra and what it is capable of when open?" asked A'na. Lucy sat motionless and was pondering all that A'na had just told her about our third eye chakra. She muttered, "amazing! A'na, I think that it is truly amazing. That is why athletes, for example, go through the motion of their pitches, dives, or skiing down a snow-covered slope in their mind's eye. They can see themselves doing these things and the mind is in agreement with their vision." "Oh wow, you do get it, Lucy!" Said A'na in a very happy voice. The mind is in control of the body, its thoughts, and its actions. Let's say you believed you were claustrophobic. If you believe this every time you got in a space, you perceived as small you would feel very uncomfortable, but now let's say you have been hypnotized and now believe you are no longer claustrophobic, the tight spaces would no longer bother you because you believed this in your mind. You no longer reacted to small spaces because you think someone "cured" you of your claustrophobia. A hypnotic suggestion to your mind in a relaxed state.

When there is a blockage of the third eye chakra one may notice signs of tension in the brow area, headaches and eye strain or blurred vision, sinus issues, hearing problems, and or dizziness. A blocked or sluggish sixth chakra is not uncommon because we tend to live in the head, logical mind, a place of logic.

When the sixth chakra is open and/or balanced, we tend to have self-awareness, self-reflection, inner vision, and focus. We are able to see the truth. We will have good visualization skills, the ability to recall dreams, pattern recognition, psychic perception, clear thoughts, the ability to contemplate, good memory, and intuition.

Eating foods high in omega3, walnuts, salmon, chia seeds, sardines, and dark chocolate will aid in opening the sixth chakra. The essential oils of palo santo, jasmine, melissa, rose, chamomile, and geranium all aid in freeing a blocked or sluggish third eye chakra. Wearing the crystals, fluorite, purple amethyst, sodalite, lapis lazuli, azurite, dumortierite, labradorite, iolite, and black obsidian. Last, but not least, dancing allows us complete freedom. We are able to get out of our heads. With this freedom, we are more open and balanced, our third eye chakra becomes more open and balanced.

Positive Affirmations for the Third Eye Chakra:

It is now safe for me to express my feelings and to create the life I deserve.

I trust my intuition.
I nurture my spirit.
I forgive myself.
I am open to inspiration and peace.
The Crown Chakra

The seventh chakra is called the crown chakra. It is located above the crown of the head and acts as the center of spirit. The Sanskrit word for the crown chakra is Sahasrara or "Crown." This chakra has a unique role in your human spiritual connection and consciousness. It is known as "the bridge to the cosmos." It is the most spiritual chakra. This chakra governs the interaction and communication with the universe, one's sense of inspiration and devotion, union with the higher self and the Divine and deeper understanding and is responsible for a happy spiritual life. Its color is violet or white. The element of the crown chakra is thought. Its symbol is a circle with a thousand petals. This chakra allows for experiences of unity and universal connectedness. It is considered masculine energy.

When the crown chakra is blocked or out of alignment, we experience difficulty feeling connected, we have difficulty meditating, there is spiritual disinterest, boredom. We feel antsy with the mundane. We may not feel connected to our purpose in this life or that we have wisdom. Sometimes there is a desire for complete isolation. Depression, apathy, skepticism, sarcasm, and narrow-mindedness are all signs of a blocked crown chakra.

Visualization, lying upside down, EFT (Emotional Freedom Techniques) from tapping on certain spots on the body, acupuncture, and other alternative treatments for physical pain and emotional stress are all ways to align and or unblock the crown chakra. Fasting is considered spiritual nourishment for the seventh chakra. The essential oils of lavender and jasmine are considered to be calming and soothing, Cedarwood, sandalwood, frankincense, and myrrh can be stimulating for the crown chakra. Crystals that clear the crown chakra are clear quartz, selenite, and diamonds for releasing energy and bringing illumination. Purple stones like apophyllite, sugilite, and amethyst will also clear any negative energy.

Positive Affirmations for the Crown Chakra: I honor my spirit and the Divine within me. I have access to wisdom and peace.

I am guided by something greater than myself.
I am connected to the universe and to everything around me.
I am healed on all levels of my being.
I am fully aware and awake.
I am open to letting go of my attachments.
I am connected to all that is.

Lucy, this is the summary of the seven main chakras. I want you to know and realize that each chakra plays an important role in empowering you to be your best self. As you acknowledge your connection to something greater, it allows you to approach your life with purpose. We, all of us, receive Divine Inspiration and have a broader perspective for life through our chakras. Namaste' (The light in me honors the light in you). Remember, everything is energy!

Lucy, by now you have realized that the first guided meditation I took you on was a chakra clearing journey. From my perspective, you not only got to have your first meditation but got to clear your chakras at the same time. As we walked in, among, and through each colored field of flowers, each of your chakras was receiving a dose of color, helping to open and align your chakras. We teach the children on Mentaka a mnemonic or acronym to remember the colors of the seven main chakras: Roy G. Biv (red, orange, yellow, green, blue, indigo, and violet). The beautiful colors of the rainbows are all over the universe. Colors, like everything else, are energy, and that energy affects us in subtle ways. The spiritual world is one of subtleties. One has to set one's intention to be aware, to feel, and to know beyond what the eyes are seeing. "Remember Lucy, there are no mistakes, only opportunities. The Universe conspires to inspire! It is all good, even the bad." said A'na with a big smile on her face. She had wanted to remind Lucy of this often so that she may reflect on what she was saying without saying it. Lucy would have to read between the lines, and she was becoming quite good at doing just that. Lucy had come so far from where she was when she had first met A'na. Did she know how far she had come? A'na was excited for her and the growth she had seen in her in so many ways!

Chapter 14

Having Some Fun

"Lucy, I think you have been exposed to much today and it is probably time you head back home before it gets too late. What would you think about a little excursion tomorrow? Just you and me getting out and about in your locale?" inquired A'na. Lucy was quiet and seemed distracted by all that had been shared this day, and yet she heard every word A'na had said and was already putting a plan together. "A'na, I have an idea. How would you like to ride horseback with me into town and go to the Festival by the River and visit the Arboretum?" asked Lucy.

Lucy knew that no one could see A'na and even if they did, it really wouldn't matter. They could ride double on Iris. A'na could get in the river for a nice swim, and she could go to the Arboretum and see some very beautiful roses and other flowers. She thought this would be something that would really make A'na happy. "Lucy, I think that is a great idea. What fun!" A'na exclaimed. They hugged one another and agreed to meet at Lucy's house at 10 o'clock.

It was really hard to tell which one was giddier and more excited about their journey tomorrow. Both Lucy and A'na had big smiles on their faces. Lucy headed toward home. She had a million thoughts in her head but reminded herself to blow them away and just skip and sing. She looked up above the tree line into the big beautiful blue sky. She looked all around her and heard the birds singing and turned around to see that some of the woodland creatures were escorting her towards home. She felt very happy, safe, and secure. She felt at peace, something she had not felt in a while. Although she had always believed in God, she now had a broader perspective of what she thought God is. She felt she belonged in this world and had a purpose for being here at this time. She had realized that she was part of something greater and she belonged. She had A'na to thank for her newfound beliefs and perspectives. Although nothing had really changed about her world, she felt everything was so different. It was she who had changed from the inside out. Her world would never be the same. The pandemic no longer scared her. She did not fear her own death and now knew that it was out of her hands, she just had to believe and trust that it was all good. She believed in our Source, God in a deeper and more profound way. She would just have to step out of the way and know that the Universe really does conspire to inspire and had she been inspired over the past few months. A'nas appearance in her world had changed everything and the timing could not have been more perfect. And although Lucy knew that it was orchestrated on the other side she was in awe. She was thankful. She was more than thankful, she was humbled. She knew that her purpose in life was her journey to help others find their peace, to assist them in finding hope, and leading others to our new way of life that is on the horizon. Lucy found herself to be very happy. She was content to know the spiritual truths that A'na had shared. She needed no proof for it was already in her own spiritual heart. Her life would be forever changed thanks to A'na's visit.

Lucy got home and spent some time with the horses, telling Iris that she was going to be needed for a ride into town tomorrow morning. She gave each horse their grain and a bit of hay for the evening. She then turned and went in for the day, putting her journal and recorder away. She helped her mother to prepare supper and set the table. As the family sat down for their evening meal it was obvious to her mother that Lucy was in a very good mood, happy. Lucy appeared happier than her mother had seen her in a long, long, time. She smiled at Lucy and asked, "So tell me what has gotten you so happy?" her mother asked. "Oh I am just excited I am going to ride Iris to the "Festival by the River" if that is OK with you and dad?" she asked. Lucy didn't ask her parents for much and although they were a bit reluctant to let her go by herself, they agreed she could go if she kept her distance from everyone and wore her mask. She gave them both a big hug before they sat down to eat their dinner. There was little chit-chat, as both her parents were tired from working at their jobs. Lucy turned in early. She knew that tomorrow would be a big day! She knew she would be too excited to sleep much as she was ready for the morning.

A'na got back to her ship in time to do her sunset meditation. She prepared her blanket and laid it on the ground just so. She grounded herself, although she had, as usual, already grounded herself several times that day. She sat cross-legged on the blanket as the woodland creatures were nearby observing and keeping an eye out for anyone that may stray her way. She was very happy and content. She knew that for whatever reason, she was meant to land her ship on planet Earth and she was also meant to meet Lucy and share her spiritual knowledge. She also knew Lucy was a special one, an old soul. She could feel it and knew it to be so. They shared a kindred spirit and it warmed A'nas' heart. She loved this young girl. A'na knew that Lucy's light would be greatly needed as things would get much worse before they would begin to get better. Humanity was at a crossroads, and much was coming to the surface. She reminded herself that it was part of the journey for Mother Earth. There would be much more turmoil, death, illness, and hard times. Although Earth was destined to move forward and be a fifth-dimensional planet, there were many who would not make that journey with her. There would be dark times ahead for planet Earth. A'na pulled herself back to her meditation. She centered herself and focused on her breath. She took several deep relaxing breaths and she set her intent on being thankful. She went deep within and communicated with her higher self. There was nothing she could ever hide from her higher self for she is aware this is a part of her being that has been with her throughout all of her sojourns from the beginning. The Higher Self knows her better than she may know herself, even coming from and living on a fifth-dimensional planet. A'na knows the psyche is a trickster sometimes and will try to make one see or not see things that are before our eyes as a way of protection. A'na felt like she was on the verge of knowing something and did not know what it was. She knew if she tried too hard to retrieve this information it would slip further and further away. She would have to let it come to her when she was ready to receive. She sat in silent meditation for over an hour, sending out her love and her gratitude. As A'na opened her eyes she saw the woodland creatures in a circle around her. They were her safety net while on planet Earth. She nodded and smiled at the creatures then stood and stretched, then sat back down on her blanket with the woodland friends nearby. A'na loved having their company. She appreciated their love and respect. She looked up at the stars fondly, remembering life on Mentaka, the beauty of the planet and the life she had left behind, for a while at least.

A'na too, turned in early this night as she also knew there was a big day coming tomorrow. She was excited to just have some fun with young Lucy. She looked forward to riding upon Iris and especially getting into the water for a swim! She arose early to prepare for and do her sunrise meditation before heading out to meet Lucy. She felt great happiness at having Lucy come into her life and had learned much from her interactions with Lucy.

She had observed great love, compassion, and respect from Lucy and knew she was an old soul with a great mission. She was glad and grateful for being a small part of Lucy's mission. A'na did not realize how big a part of Lucy's mission she was, neither of them did. Both, A'na and Lucy's lives were about to change forever.

A'na arrived at Lucy's house just as planned. The woodland creatures walked with A'na to the edge of the woods. The woodland creatures knew they could go no further without causing a scene. A'na assured them that she and Lucy would be fine and would see them later on in the day. They understood and retreated back to the edge of the woods. Lucy was just heading out the door to wait on A'na's arrival. They greeted one another and headed toward the barn to put a halter on Iris, and both agreed they would ride her bareback to the event if Iris was in agreement. A'na took a moment to "speak" with Iris, as Lady Reno, Spirit, Sami and the new baby horse, Bell, all chimed in with a nicker to greet A'na. She introduced herself to all of them as she asked Iris if they could have her permission to ride on her back to the event in town. Iris perked up her ears and listened intently as A'na told her that they wanted to ride bareback which pleased Iris. It wasn't clumsy feeling like a saddle. Iris felt honored that she was able to communicate with A'na and relayed to her that she knew Lucy really loved her, all of them and had taken good care of them. A'na told Lucy what Iris had communicated to her. It put a smile on Lucy's face as she rubbed Iris upon the withers. Lucy gently got onto Iris' back, followed by A'na and they headed out for their journey. It would take them about twenty minutes by horseback to get to the festival. They saw several cars along the way and Lucy waved to several friends she saw. She knew she could talk with A'na telepathically without saying a word with her mouth. Lucy thought to herself that was pretty cool. "I can hear you, Lucy," A'na whispered and snickered to herself.

Iris told A'na she had been communicating telepathically all her life as a horse, but no one seemed to really notice. "Iris, I'm sorry. Many of the humans are still asleep and are not aware that you or any of the other creatures can communicate telepathically, or just how intelligent you really are, but hopefully, things will be changing sooner than later," replied A'na. Iris let A'na know that she understood and looked forward to the day when things changed, and all of the animals and humans could really interact as a family.

Lucy said, "Iris Athena is her full name." Iris is a big, beautiful, red, quarter horse. Her body is muscular, well-shaped, and toned. She has big brown eyes that could peer into your soul. She has a beautiful white blaze on her face. It extends above her right eye at the brow bone and down the center of her face, only adding to her beauty. It is the shape of the number one. She is the second youngest of the herd at 12 years of age. She is also the alpha mare for her group of several horses. She slipped into the role of alpha mare after her much-loved companion, Chico, passed. She had stood by his side as like a bodyguard, as 2nd in command, even leaving her mare's side to be with him. Chico was a very tall, dark chocolate, almost black, Tennessee Walking horse. He had been trained and shown hard until he was let go because of his age. He lived to be forty years old or more per the veterinarian. Iris adored Chico. It was so obvious. After his passing, it was only natural that she takes over as the alpha mare. Iris is very self-assured and leads her herd in a diplomatic way. She is stern when needed but she is also laid back and does not get overly stressed by anything. She has a sense of humor and a natural curiosity to match. She "helped" to build our new corral and has helped repair several fences and slow feeders with my dad. Iris always comes in first to see any new visitors, animals or humans. She is very intelligent. Iris is the only horse that eats her feed with her head in the air so as not to lose a morsel. At the age of three, she was trained to ride under saddle in an afternoon.

The trainer, Martinez, refers to her as "Big Red," a powerhouse of a horse who has breathtaking speed. Bell was brought into the herd for Iris, she too is a dark chocolate Tennessee Walking horse. She looks much like Chico and because of this it will comfort Iris as her dam, Lady Reno makes her transition in the near future. Lady Reno was born pigeon-toed, a condition that was never corrected and as result she has had much of her body weight placed on her knees, causing swelling, arthritis and much pain for her.

Lucy, A'na, and Iris arrived at the festival and decided they would walk Iris around a bit before tying her to a tree for safety, hers and others. A'na telepathically assured Iris she would be fine and that she and Lucy would not be gone long. Lucy and A'na walked to a sandy area by the river's edge and quickly entered the water. This was a very, very refreshing and beautiful treat for A'na. After all, she was used to being in the water every day on her planet. She swam, she floated, she dove, she stood, and she enjoyed the feeling of water upon her skin. The fishes were already swimming all around her. The word had gotten out to the fishes and to all the nature creatures that one who could talk with them was close by. A'na looked at the edge of the woods where she could see a few of woodland creatures hiding. She again reassured her friends she was fine and "said" hello to some new friends, welcoming them. She also "said" hello to the fishes, telling them how beautiful they were and how happy she was to meet them and see them.

After about an hour in the water, Lucy asked A'na if she would like to go into the Arboretum. A'na said, "Yes, of course, I would love to. Let me dry for a few minutes before we enter, please." The Arboretum was completely open and had a fence around the exterior perimeter of it. There was a pretty white fence around four feet tall to help keep the local pets out of the garden area. As they went through the main entrance Lucy thought she saw one of the rose bushes turn slightly and nod to A'na. The rose bush had several big, rather large blooms. A'na whispered to Lucy, "It is called a Peace Rose." The blooms were a beautiful shade of yellow, edged in pink. The fragrance caught your attention upon entering the arboretum. She was a big beautiful rose bush with glossy deep green leaves. Lucy watched A'na cradle several of the blooms in her hands. She was obviously saying words of kindness and respect. She had to shake her head a bit and giggle. Amazing, she thought, just amazing. She was pleased to be witness to such a beautiful action and honored to be with A'na and call her a friend. Although Lucy was a young girl, she understood the effect that A'na had not only on herself but all other living beings for they could feel it too. She had such great love in her heart that it sent out nothing but love and those vibrations felt so wonderful, warm, and accepting. Lucy thought for a moment and told herself it was like her mother's love, love without conditions. A'na made you feel like you had a warm blanket around you on a cold day. Lucy could be herself around A'na without any pretense, without any worry of being judged. It was such a wonderful feeling to be near her.

Once into the arboretum A'na and Lucy went from plant to plant and although she could not hear what A'na was saying to the plants she knew it was loving appreciation, encouragement, and gratitude. Lucy watched as A'na lovingly caressed all of the plants, taking them gently into her palms and acknowledging each one, thanking them for their beautiful gifts. It was a beautiful experience that Lucy would never ever forget. Lucy and A'na were both glowing from the inside. The plants would never forget their experience either, being acknowledged in such a loving and respectful way. "Word" would be sent from these plants to all the other plants in the vicinity and beyond. A'na's love was better than any fertilizer that could be used on these plants.

It had been a fun day for both the girls, and they decided that it was time to head back before it got too late. Iris had been moved by one of the arboretum caretakers and placed in a small fenced-in area where she could move about while Lucy and A'na had some fun together. When they got back to Iris, A'na took a minute to "speak" with Iris and thank her for allowing them to ride upon her back and providing transportation. Lucy saw Iris relax a bit and lift her head with her ears turned in. She had understood completely what A'na was saying to her and responded in kind. She put her legs out in front of her and lowered herself as if bowing to allow the girls to get up on her back with less effort. Once on her back, Iris gently stood up. Lucy gave Iris a gentle nudge with her knees and cluck with her lips signaling Iris they were ready to begin their ride back. Iris decided to take a little time to canter and show off her skills and then eased into a gentle walk. The girls held on, giggling and laughing as they enjoyed the ride back to Lucy's house.

As they returned, they both noticed that Lucy's parents were home early. A'na reassured Lucy and told her to just act normal. She reminded Lucy that her parents cannot see her either. Lucy took in a breath and relaxed as she brought Iris to a halt. Iris again stretched her front legs out and lowered herself so that the two could more easily dismount from her back. "Wow, when did you teach Iris to do that trick for you?" asked Lucy's father. Lucy laughed, "It was something she did herself daddy."

A'na was laughing at the question Lucy's father asked. She then turned and thanked Iris as she jumped off to the ground. Lucy then led Iris back to the barn where she removed her halter and also thanked her for a beautiful ride to and from the festival while hugging her neck. Iris quickly ran and joined the other horses in the pasture who were looking and waiting to hear all about Iris' adventure.

A'na turned and gave Lucy a big hug and thanked her for such a fun day. She then made her way back into the forest where the woodland creatures soon appeared to escort her back to her spacecraft. It was a wonderful walk home. There was a gentle breeze in the air that seemed to kiss A'nas skin as she walked on the woodland path. She breathed in deeply as she took in the scenery nearby. She had time to walk in the creek for a few minutes and reflect and appreciate her day with Lucy at the Arboretum before heading to her spacecraft. It was a very special day for the two, one she will never forget. Ana invited her animal friends to come and join her in the water. Several of the foxes entered the water followed by two raccoons. Several of the birds flew onto the lower branches allowing them to flitter in and out of the water. After a while, A'na got out of the creek and back onto the path towards her ship. It wasn't long before she had arrived. She sat on the ground and looked up into the sky knowing that her time with Lucy was coming to an end before too long. She shared her thoughts with the woodland creatures as they had become family to her as well. They were saddened she would be leaving someday soon but understood that she needed to go back to her planet and her home on Mentaka. They communicated with A'na telling her how much they loved her and how they would miss her communicating with them every day and sharing her thoughts with them. They would miss her respect and love, her compassion and understanding. A'na brought out some fruit and nuts that Lucy had brought her some time ago and shared it with all who were there with her. After some time she prepared to do her sunrise meditation as the creatures again remained as her lookouts. She spread out her blanket and sat cross-legged, deeply breathing in and then out. She entered her meditation with ease and sat silently for over an hour and a half. She came out of her meditation just as easily, standing up and stretching. She looked around to see her friends nearby and thanked them for standing by. She said good night to all of them as she was going into the ship for the evening to enter some thoughts into the palm pilot before retiring. She fell asleep very quickly and had beautiful dreams of Mentaka. She saw her family and even her sister Raina was there. She and Raina were laughing and smiling. She could see her face clearly and the smile that was very apparent. They were at a celebration. All were laughing and having a good time. People were dancing. The children were laughing and playing.

Healing Herbs

Lucy, I think you may enjoy our next subject as it too, is dear and near to my heart and that subject is, herbs. Herbs are a beautiful alternative to man-made chemicals that your planet has used for some time now. Pills that are called medicine, but to me they are forms of poison to the body. They may treat the symptoms, but not the cause. Your planet has a very large pharmaceutical presence and along with it a very big money trail. It is very easy to pop a pill in your mouth and think that it is helping you. Remember what I have taught you about holding onto your emotions? If you can learn to have the emotions and let it go it will not settle in your body to fester. There may be a time in your future that you may need to have or use herbs. There are hundreds of herbs on your planet and mine, but we are going to start slowly as this is something you can research on your own. A'na had thought that Lucy may have some fun learning about herbs in her area of Mother Earth and thought that she could invite several of her friends into the woods by the creek as she taught Lucy about some of those herbs and the properties of essential oils. After all, they could not see A'na nor could they hear her, and she could easily hear Lucy's questions and comments telepathically. Lucy listened as A'na made her suggestions about inviting some of her friends. She thought about it for a while and then replied to A'na. "I will do it." she said. I will invite several of my closest friends, Jean, Lauren, Debbie, Phyllis, Cathy, Rebecca, Judy, Sherry, Ann, and Monica. These were the friends Lucy could go to if she needed a friend to listen to her or to help her if needed. We can have snacks and fruit and have some fun. You're right A'na, they cannot see you or hear you and if I forget something about the herbs you will be right there to guide me. Thank you A'na." "Why are you thanking me Dear One?" inquired A'na. "Because you are always thinking of me and helping me in so many ways." replied Lucy. A'na looked at Lucy with a big smile.

In preparation for the event, A'na and Lucy spent the rest of the day looking for and gathering several herbs that were close in proximity. A'na gathered about five different herbs and began explaining what they were and the properties that they have. She had the same herbs on her planet. Lucy was very focused and intent on learning about the herbs. A'na thought that they could even make some salves and balms eventually. These were the ways of the indigenous people on your planet, Lucy. It was the indigenous people that have kept this knowledge and the spiritual knowledge from generation to generation by word of mouth. Much of this knowledge has been lost, as humanity has gone in and out of enlightenment, but alas, I see that there has been a renewed interest in much of the lost knowledge and natural remedies that are still available. It is a beautiful day to talk with and collect some our herbal friends.

"Lucy, while we are out in the natural world on this beautiful sunny, clear day, there is something I want to show you, something you have been very interested in. Come over here close to me I want you to look up into the sky. Just relax and let your mind wander while you are not looking at anything in particular. It is a perfect sunny day. This is when you can see the mana in the air, floating about. It almost looks like tiny insects flittering about inside of air bubbles." A'na explained. Lucy was quiet for a moment while she looked into the sunny sky above her. She found herself seeing the mana in no time at all, as she yelled out, "They have lights inside of their bubbles!" Lucy was awe struck and had a smile on her face.

"Come, Lucy," said A'na. The two headed out towards an open area. It wasn't long before A'na said, "Stop, here is the first herb I want to introduce you to. This is the dandelion." "I am familiar with the dandelion. We used to pick their little wispy things when I was small. We would blow on them and watch as the little pieces went into the air." explained Lucy. I am sure you are familiar with the dandelion. Most on your planet think of the dandelion as just a weed, something that is invasive, taking up space in all the pretty manicured lawns and not wanted. The dandelion has many medicinal properties. It can be brewed as a tea and drank, or it can be used in or as a salad. Its properties include providing antioxidants, reducing cholesterol, regulating blood sugar, reducing inflammation, lowering blood pressure, aiding in weight loss, reducing cancer risks, and boosting the immune system. The tea may soothe digestive issues. "Oh wow, I didn't realize it had so many useful properties! I will never look at the dandelion in the same way." vowed Lucy.

Lucy was enjoying learning about the herbs. She watched as A'na gently bent down and caressed the plant before picking it. She was sure she had spoken some very kind and loving words to it and had asked permission to pick it. Lucy had a smile on her face as she looked on with curiosity.

Ok, here we go, let us continue. Here is our next herb. This second herb is called Stinging Nettle or just Nettle. It grows in open areas or pastures. It is dark green. It may have a red or purplish tinge to the leaves. Small hairs grow on the leaf that do sting and may cause a painful rash when touched. Soaking the nettles in water for ten minutes removes the irritants. It needs to be collected with gloves. One must use care when working with stinging nettle. It can be dried and then steeped in water and made into a tea to be drunk for allergies or allergic reactions. It is a good herb to keep on hand. Nettle tea has an abundance of vitamins, minerals, and phytonutrients. It can also be added to a variety of foods and dishes as fresh leaves.

Stinging nettle helps to maintain urinary tract health and it can relieve prostate swelling. The diuretic effects of nettle assist in flushing out the bladder and urinary tract to prevent infection and kidney stones.

The third herb we are finding is Yarrow. It is a member of the aster family. It has flat-topped clusters of small blooms. You may recognize this herb from yarrow growing in your mom's garden. It also grows wild. We want to find yarrow that is white, pink, or light purple. Yarrow also grows along roadsides and in meadows. You want to collect it while in bloom. Yarrow grows to be about 3 feet in height. It is a perennial. Its aromatic, fine, feathery-cut leaves give it a fern like appearance.

Yarrow induces sweating and stops wound bleeding. It reduces heavy menstrual bleeding and pain and helps to relieve gastrointestinal ailments. It has been used for cerebral and coronary thrombosis, to lower high blood pressure, improve circulation, and tone various veins.

The Greek name for yarrow is Achillea, as it was referred to in Greek mythology. Achilles used yarrow to treat his soldier's wounds. It was chewed and used as a poultice to be placed on the wound.

Our next herb is calendula. Calendula plants stand out with bright flower petals, usually yellow or orange, their petals are described as a sunray shape. It grows 1-2 feet tall. The flower is widely used as a medicinal plant. It has antibacterial, antifungal, antimicrobial, and anti-inflammatory properties that make it a strong ingredient for healing. Calendula also has antioxidant components which may help to fight cancer, prevent heart disorders and ease muscle fatigue. A tea can be made from dried flowers and applied externally to wounds and burns or taken internally to help heal the mouth, throat, or drank to help digestive disorders. It is a good herb to have on hand. "Oh wow is it pretty!' exclaimed Lucy.

The next herb we are going to visit and collect is chamomile. Chamomile goes back to ancient times in Egypt. It was used in a variety of healing applications. It is related to the daisy family. It is about 2 feet tall and has strongly scented foliage and flowers with white petals and yellow centers.

Chamomile tea can be used as a tonic or an antiseptic and many other herbal remedies. The tea is usually made from English or Roman varieties. The tea can be used as a remedy for sleeping disorders because of its relaxing qualities. It can also be used to treat menstrual pain, diabetes, or lowering blood sugar, slowing or preventing osteoporosis, reducing inflammation, and treating cold symptoms. It can be used as a mouth rinse or as a poultice for irritation. Again A'na bent down and cupped her hands around and over some of the chamomile before she took a whiff and placed it in her collection basket.

The herb class was planned for Saturday at the creek, weather permitting. Lucy called each of the girls and told them what she had planned. She wasn't sure if they would be interested, but all were, and it was agreed to meet at Lucy's house at 11 am and they would all walk to the creek together. Lucy was excited in so many ways. She would be with her friends she knew, and she would be with A'na, although no one would know that A'na was even there, she would. She knew she must keep A'na secret until much later when the time was right, and she could be believed. In the meantime, she and A'na had some preparations to make before Saturday.

Lucy made a list of the things she would need to have ready by the creek; blankets to sit upon, fruit, snacks, and water for everyone. A'na wanted to have some of the herbs ready and dried so that Lucy could see the difference between the live plant and when it is dried. She and Lucy prepared a diagram board of the herbs and their properties. A'na wanted to make some of the herbs into salves and teas ahead of time so that Lucy could see how it is done and for the girls to try and to taste. This allowed Lucy to have more confidence leading her friends in this class and experience in working with herbs.

Lucy and A'na began by finding and locating the herbs they would be describing and locating on Saturday for the class. It would be fun and a time that was needed for the girls to be together outdoors, having fun together and learning something that could help them in the future. A'na instructed Lucy on identifying and gathering the herbs. Lucy had told the girls to each bring a pencil, garden gloves, and scissors, along with five small paper bags for collecting and labeling.

Saturday had arrived and Lucy was ready for her friends. They arrived at her house one by one, just as they had promised. After everyone was there, they made their way to the creek, talking, giggling, and acting silly. A'na was beside Lucy with a smile on her face at seeing Lucy so happy. When they got to the creek the girls saw the blankets, snacks, and water and told Lucy how pretty everything looked. They especially like her diagram board. Lucy let the girls settle in and calm down a bit before she began to tell them about herbs and how the indigenous people used them before chemicals and pills were our way of life. She explained how "Mother Earth" has all of the medicine we need within her array of plants and how we could use them for our everyday needs without using and putting chemicals into our bodies. She explained how we were used to seeing our family and our friends take medicine and pills for everything and that someday it would be different and how we would realize that. She even went on to say how the big pharmaceutical companies were making money hand over fist selling their "medicine," or rather chemicals in disguise.

The girls clapped and applauded Lucy for her information and began whispering to one another. Lucy looked a little puzzled and was a bit concerned about what was going on. She asked, "Is everything OK?" Debbie replied, "Yes we were just talking about how you have changed. You seem so confident." "Oh," Lucy said while looking at A'na who was by her side. She asked the girls to join her on a little trip to find some herbs." "Don't forget your pencils, paper bags and scissors," she instructed them.

Lucy, A'na, and the girls were out in the woods, the edge of the woods, and in the open areas for about an hour, finding, looking at, and gathering herbs. It was fun and they seemed quite happy on their mission. Each of the girls had their bags full of fresh herbs and all were headed back to the creek and were almost back when Monica had her leg cut by some saw briars. She squealed out in pain and grabbed her leg to get the briars to disengage. Blood was inking through her pants. A'na grabbed Lucy by the arm, remembering they have something for that at the creek, the salve we had made. Lucy thought, oh yeah, the calendula. It will be perfect for Monica's briar cuts. Lucy told Monica she had something to help her at the creek. As soon as they got there Lucy went to the container she had and pulled out the balm she had A'na had made earlier in the week. She asked Monica if she could apply some of the balm to her cuts as Monica was shaking her head "yes." Monica lifted her pants leg, and it was apparent some of the saw briars were still in her skin between her socks and her pedal pushers, where there was bare skin. Lucy carefully pulled each one out as Monica winced in pain. She dampened a paper towel to cleanse the area and then she applied the calendula balm to Monica's leg. The girls had already encircled Monica and wanted to see what Lucy was doing and what she had in her hands. Within moments the bleeding had stopped, and Monica said she was feeling fine. Lucy told Monica and the others that she had made a balm earlier in the week with the calendula she had dried. She explained how this particular herb helped to prevent infection and helps to heal injuries. Lucy also explained that it could be made into a tea that could be applied to external wounds and drink to heal mouth, throat, and digestive issues. Everyone had stopped what they were doing and were looking at Lucy with their mouths open. Debbie said, "Wow, who are you?" Lucy was caught off guard and seemed to flush pink with embarrassment. I'm sorry I just get excited about the herbs and what they can do for us. A'na was snickering and felt like a proud mama watching Lucy taking care of another and teaching as well. She had obviously done her homework. A'na had nothing to add except, Well done Lucy!

After a while, the girls settled in and were now learning about each of the other herbs and their properties. Monica's leg was a great learning moment, not that Lucy wanted anyone to get hurt. Lucy seemed to love sharing her knowledge about the herbs and A'na knew she would carry on with learning about the many other herbs and making teas, balms, and tinctures. She had no doubt. As the afternoon came to an end Lucy, A'na, and the girls all walked back to Lucy's house. They thanked Lucy for the fun time and the herbal knowledge they would now have. She gave them the name of some of her favorite websites for herbs and herbal recipes.

After waiting for the girls to make their departure, A'na gave Lucy a hug as she was about to head out to her meadow and spacecraft. A'na told her she would see her in a few days. "How does Monday morning sound?" Lucy asked. "That sounds great!" replied A'na. She turned and headed towards the path to the creek where once again she was greeted by the woodland creatures who had been hiding ever so closely watching everything that had taken place. A'na and the creatures walked together on the path to A'na's spacecraft. The sun would soon be setting soon as A'na quickly prepared for her sunset meditation. The woodland creatures watched quietly as A'na laid out her blanket. She sat down and crossed her legs one over the other. She took in a big breath and closed her eyes as she let out her breath. She took in several deeper breaths as she found herself transported to another place. She was sitting under a huge tree; the air was filled with a purple mist. She saw Raina was standing off in the distance. She had stood up and was heading in her direction when she realized she was back on the ground in front of her spacecraft. It shook her a bit, but she had a feeling she could not describe. She felt that her sister was there with her, but she could not touch her or go to her. She could just see her in her mind's eye. A'na knew there was a deeper meaning in this visit but could not figure it out. Raina would always be in her heart. She reminded herself, love is eternal. Love lives in eternity.

A'na continued to sit upon the blanket reflecting on the day's events, her time with Lucy and the girls. She thought about how Lucy had changed to the girls and wondered if Lucy had even realized how much she had changed over the past several months. A'na looked up to see the woodland creatures nearby and looking at her with concern in their heart. She knew they had sensed her emotions when thinking of Raina. She invited them to come closer and be by her side. She assured them she was OK. She also told them how much she loved them and their loving companionship. They sat quietly and comfortably as A'na looked up at the stars. She was very grateful for the woodland creatures' company and for them. They had made her visit so much more enjoyable. She also assured them that they would all meet again someday. The creatures thanked A'na for her kind words and gentle reassurances. They agreed and also knew that they would meet again! They loved A'na and understood too that love is eternal. As A'na stood up, the creatures headed back into the woods until the morning where they would be waiting on A'na at the edge of the woods. A'na told all "Good night." As she headed into her ship for the evening, she began thinking back on all that she and Lucy had talked about, the things she had shared with Lucy, and her spiritual truths. She somehow knew that their time together would be shorter than longer, and it put a pain in her heart to leave that sweet girl she had come to love so much. She also knew in her heart that it was meant to be this way and she would somehow be back on her planet Mentaka and with her family. She drifted off into sound sleep and awoke to the darkness just before dawn with a smile on her face. She had reminded herself how grateful she was to be in such a wonderful place and surrounded by the most astonishing woodland creatures and that sweet girl, Lucy. A'na loved to teach others, it filled a spot in her heart. She prepared for her sunrise meditation. As she exited the ship, she saw her friends sitting quietly at the edge of the woods. They were all present and on lookout for any intruders. This morning she had decided to set her intent to feel unconditional love in her heart, the love of the ONE. She sat cross-legged and began breathing in deep breaths. As she breathed out the fourth time she again was transported to the same place as before, under a big tree. She opened her eyes and she saw the purple mist yet again, surrounding her, her sister Raina, was in the distance but a little closer to her. She was afraid to move because she did not want it to end. She sat quietly and observed all of it, Raina, the purple air, the tree she was sitting under, and then she noticed something way far off in the background, it was the "Cave of Rebirth." She blinked her eyes, and she was back on her blanket sitting cross-legged. She again had tears in her eyes. She wasn't exactly sure what it meant but she knew she would remember and know what all of it meant when the time was right. Raina's visit had a special meaning of some kind.

Chapter 16

Seeing is Believing

It was another beautiful day and A'na was going to meet Lucy at the creek around 10 am that morning. She started out early towards the creek. All of her friends joined with her. They walked and enjoyed each other's company. The birds were singing loudly and fluttering about from branch to branch, darting back and forth and up and down like the birds were so precise in their air patterns and could change direction in a split second. It seemed everyone was in a particularly good mood this morning. The air felt crisp and smelled clean from the rain of last night. It was like everything had been refreshed, including A'na. After arriving at the creek A'na sat and waited on Lucy to join her. She thought about sharing some crystal knowledge with Lucy and knew she would like to learn about crystals. She also knew that Lucy would like to see her spacecraft as she had not done so. She had expressed interest in seeing it and thought that maybe today would be a good day for her and Lucy to make the trek back to her spacecraft together.

As Lucy arrived, she and A'na gave each other a hug. "Lucy, how would you like to take a long trek and come see my ship?," A'na asked. "Really?!, Lucy asked, with a big-eyed grin on her face. I would love to see it!" Lucy could not stop grinning. Although she believed it was there, she had eagerly awaited to see the spacecraft with her own eyes. She was ecstatic. She had longed to see A'na's ship and could not wait. They gathered up their things and headed onto the path towards A'na's ship. It had taken about an hour, but they had made it to the edge of the woods and there waiting was the spacecraft. Lucy stood there with her mouth open for a few minutes. She was kind of in disbelief and had to stop and take it the sight that was before her eyes, a spacecraft, not just any spacecraft, it was A'na's spacecraft. She was silent. She began by walking all around it not once, but twice. She then asked A'na if she could touch it. A'na was smiling and answered, "Yes, of course, you can touch it." Lucy put her hand onto the shiny surface and held it there for a few moments. She then went around it again with her hand on its surface. "A'na it is so smooth," Lucy said, almost in a whisper. She stopped at the door hatch and looked at the emblem. "May I touch the emblem, A'na?" she asked. "Sure dear one, you may." Lucy took her index finger and traced the emblem. It was the infinity symbol with a heart in the top of it, above it was A'na's name. She then did the same with A'na's name. She was smiling and giddy and at the same time serious. "Oh, this is amazing! she said almost in a trembling from excitement. A'na, it is so beautiful! It looks like a mirror. It is so small, much smaller than I imagined, and it is more beautiful than I imagined. It has your name on it. And the emblem, what does it mean?

Lucy had been so taken aback by seeing the ship she had not even noticed the four very large quartz crystals lying on the ground. When she turned around, she had almost tripped over one of them and looked down to see all four of them before her eyes. "On my gosh! Oh my gosh! These are the crystals that pilot your ship, aren't they?" Lucy exclaimed. Yes, that is the four main crystals. You will notice the complete fracture in this one as A'na pointed to the largest crystal in the bunch and a partial fracture in this one. "A'na, can I touch the crystals?" asked Lucy. "Yes, of course, you can." replied A'na. Lucy bent down to touch one of the crystals. She was startled, she felt a tingle in her hand and jumped back. She almost felt like she was having a déjà vu experience like she had touched them before. But how could she have touched them before? She had just seen them for the first time. They are so big and so beautiful, Lucy thought aloud. But A'na why are they outside? I am letting them soak up energy from the sun." Ana told Lucy. "Oh, I see," said Lucy.

But I have not answered your question about the emblem. The emblem is ever-present on our planet. It is the infinity symbol with a heart at the top of it. It represents eternal life and eternal love. It is yet another way to remind those on our planet that we are eternal beings of light, and our love is eternal. We are just using the physical vessel to maneuver in a denser vibrational environment, just as you are on your planet, Lucy. Although our vessel seems a bit less dense than the one you use on planet Earth. Remember someday we will all drop our vessel and let our spirit self return home for our next journey.

The ship was a gift to me about 8 years ago. It was presented to me for my service to the planet and her inhabitants. It too is a gift of love. I am very fond of it as it has served me well over the years. It is made from a special alloy that is present on the planet and is equipped with every instrument I could ever need. The special alloy is what gives the mirrored appearance on the exterior.

"Lucy, would you like to go inside and take a look? asked A'na. "Oh man, would I." Lucy replied instantly. A'na stood before the door, and it immediately opened. Lucy's mouth was again open. A'na had her arm outreached, inviting Lucy to enter. Lucy took a few steps in and began looking around. She was again pleasantly surprised by the size of it. It seemed so large when inside of it. You could see from every window, 360 degrees.

Lucy imagined herself flying in A'na's ship and thought the view had to be amazing. Amazing! She imagined seeing stars and planets up close. She imagined seeing Mother Earth from above, in space. She was so excited, she felt like she had been in A'nas' ship before this day and had seen the stars and the planets from her viewing windows. She asked if she may sit in the captain's chair. "Of course," A'na answered. She watched as Lucy carefully maneuvered around the ship looking at every detail as she noted the look of awe on her face as Lucy sat in the captain's chair. "It is so comfortable, A'na," as she cooed and awed. Lucy, it conforms to the body. It has special sensors that adjust to your body as you begin to sit down in it, like it is made just for you. The moment you sat in it; it had already made adjustments for your body. Lucy looked at the instrument panel with another level of fascination. "Oh my gosh, this is so amazing! How do I not tell anyone of this beautiful experience in my life? she asked A'na. "You will when the time is ready," A'na assured her. You will.

A'na took a seat in the passenger chair beside Lucy. "Dear One, when the time is right you will tell all of what you have experienced." declared A'na. It is part of your personal truth and your experience. I want you to know that others have come to your planet in the past and many are coming now. Your experience will help to make this occurrence seem less frightening to those who are full of fear and may wish to do harm.

Lucy, remember that fear comes in many forms and some on your planet believe that they are the only forms of intelligent life. They believe that planet Earth is the only inhabitable planet. Others may use religious beliefs and think that it is the end of the world or that a deity they have conjured up, Satan, the devil is at work, there will be many in disbelief. Fear causes many emotional reactions. Your calm resolve and understanding will go a long way in bringing comfort to those who are frightened. As more and more spacecraft will be able to be seen, chaos will ensue. There is so much change coming to your planet. Calm will be needed. Hope will be needed. Love and compassion are always needed! Always remember you are the light of the ONE! This light is always present within you. They sat silently for several minutes, each thinking about the same thing. A'na will be parting soon, somehow.

"Ok my sweet girl, we probably need to get you back to your part of the woods before it gets too late, and your parents get worried about you. Are you ready to head back? The woodland creatures and I will walk back with you." A'na stated.

As they headed towards the creek, A'na suggested that they study and learn about some of the crystals on planet Earth, that is, if you would like to, Lucy? "Yes, that would be fun." Lucy agreed excitedly. "Good. Can we meet at your house around 10 am?" asked A'na. "I will be there." said Lucy. Maybe we need to take a field trip again, suggested A'na. "Do you have any crystal stores nearby?" inquired A'na. Lucy said, "We have a crystal and gem store in the little shopping center near my house. We can walk to it." "That sounds perfect," A'na said. Both A'na and Lucy knew that they had little to no money and this trip would be for learning and information gathering only.

A'na and Lucy met as planned. As they walked and talked their way to the little shop Lucy told A'na about the crystals her grandfather had given her and asked A'na if she would like to see them when they got together the next day? "I would love to know more about them," Lucy asked. "Yes, I would love to see them, Lucy," A'na replied with a smile.

When they arrived at the little shop, only the shopkeeper was there. The two went from crystal to crystal as Lucy was picking up crystals randomly. Lucy talked to A'na, asking her telepathic questions. Lucy wanted to know how the crystals get or have energy. A'na reminded Lucy about the dimensions. Remember each dimension has certain properties in play. The crystals have their own consciousness. The crystals are in the first dimension and therefore vibrate more slowly. A'na's answer seemed to hit a note of connection for Lucy, and she began to put the dimensions into something she could understand a bit better. Lucy looked at A'na and telepathically commented, "Just like most others don't see you or hear you because your vibration is faster. You are from a fifth-dimensional planet, a higher vibrational planet." "Very good Lucy, you are starting to really understand the dimensions a bit better." A'na said with joy in her voice. A'na would verbally answer because no one could her hear but Lucy. A'na had Lucy to pick up several specific crystals and just hold them in her hand silently. A'na would first tell her about the crystal, its name and a few of the metaphysical properties it possesses. She would then ask Lucy to hold the crystal in her hand for a few moments. She asked Lucy if she felt any sensations or energy the crystal gave her while she was holding it in her hand. After spending some time with a few of the crystals A'na then asked her what she had taken away from the crystals. Lucy's eyebrows were reaching high as if she was confused. She telepathically asked A'na "What am I supposed to feel?" "Anything, everything, nothing, or something," A'na responded. "Lucy, you have to remember this is a subtle language, use your gut and your imagination to assist you. I know this is very different from what you are used to. Be gentle with yourself and allow. It may take you some time to sense these sensations or you may sense them immediately if you just allow."

After about an hour in the shop, Lucy turned to the clerk and thanked him for allowing her to look at and visit with the crystals, Lucy and A'na both turned and exited the store and headed back towards Lucy's house. A'na told Lucy it was a good visit at the shop and crystals were something she could learn about and work with throughout her life. She encouraged Lucy to have some fun with crystals and assured her she would be able to feel their energy and what they had to share with her in the very near future. Lucy looked at A'na and asked if she could bring her grandfather's crystals for her to look at tomorrow. "Tomorrow would be a good day to look at and talk about the crystals you have," said A'na. They again agreed to meet at the creek around 10 am. As Lucy went in for the evening, she collected her grandfathers' crystals and carefully wrapped and packed them into her backpack one by one so she would be ready to take them with her in the morning. Lucy was excited to learn about the crystals her grandfather had found and had given to her. He knew she loved crystals and would cherish them. She then prepared herself for bed. As she said her prayers, she realized that even they had changed. She was more aware of being grateful than asking for favors. She sleeps soundly that night and awoke refreshed and ready to learn about her crystals from A'na. She put her backpack on and headed out of the house towards the now, very worn, trail to the creek. Once there, she took let out a sigh. She wasn't really sure why, but she felt a bit anxious after arriving.

A'na was already at the creek side and waiting on Lucy. Lucy put down her backpack and they greeted each other with a hug. A'na had Lucy to ground herself as she did the same before, they began handling and looking at Lucy's crystals. A'na asked Lucy if she was ready for her to see what crystals she had. Lucy picked her backpack up. She then retrieved the first crystal that she had received from her grandfather, unwrapped it and handing it over to A'na so she could hold the crystal. A'na was astonished! This crystal immediately struck A'na's heart. Lucy this crystal is called phenacite. It is prominent on Mentaka. It is a high vibration stone. It would be the very crystal that would be able to repair A'nas' navigation crystals. Lucy had already noticed the look on A'na face and knew that something was up. A'na shared all of the information with Lucy with great excitement. Lucy had wanted to bring the crystals to A'na for quite some time and for some reason she had been reluctant to do so. Could it be that somewhere in the back of her subconscious mind she knew that this would enable A'na to repair her large navigation crystals and go back to Mentaka? Lucy felt ashamed of herself for even thinking that thought and yet she did not want A'na to leave her and go back to her own planet. She felt guilty for having those feelings. She muttered to herself and tried not to "say" her thoughts aloud. Maybe A'na had not received her thoughts telepathically, she thought. Even if she had, A'na already knew Lucy didn't want her to leave. And even as much as A'na wanted to be back on Mentaka, she did not want to leave Lucy. This child filled a place in her heart and brought her much joy!

What Lucy had not taken into consideration was the fact that A'na loved her just as much as she loved A'na. Although she would be excited about leaving to go back home to her planet Mentaka, she would miss Lucy just as much. She could not deny that she felt a deep sadness in her heart about leaving Lucy. They both tried to act like everything was OK, but it wasn't. It would be difficult for both of them to part ways.

Lucy's stone was a very clear quartz crystal about two inches long and about one inch in diameter. It appears to have, what looks like, a city skyline, not unlike one of your New York city's skyscapes or like it has had dwellings that were carved into a mountainside. The other side of the crystal is uneven but smooth. When held in the light one can see there are several rainbows within the crystal itself. She handed the crystal to Lucy so that she could see what A'na was talking about exactly.

Lucy, let me tell you about your crystal. It is very, very special! It carries the properties of quartz, and it aids in interdimensional travel. It also helps and facilitates accessing vibratory spiritual states that would normally not be reached from earth. It activates memories of earlier spiritual initiations and teaches that "like attracts like," urging you to raise your vibrations, purify your thoughts, and put out positive energy. Lucy the spirit of this stone is profoundly joyful and teaches that life, and spiritual evolution should be fun. It is an extremely powerful activator for the crown chakra. It produces a "fountain effect" in which golden energy pours in from the highest realms of being.

Lucy was listening intently and was again, awed. She had a smile on her face and was very honored to have such a profound crystal in her possession. She would take very good care of it and put it in a place of honor in her room. She did not know it but someday she would meditate with this very crystal on a daily basis and wear it on her person each day. She and this crystal would be lifelong friends and partners. It would aid her consciousness in profound ways that she could not yet imagine.

"Lucy, let's look at the other crystals you have brought for me to see," said A'na. Lucy retrieved another crystal from her backpack. She carefully handed them, one by one to A'na. The second crystal was called Candle Quartz, it is another high vibration stone. It is named so because it looks like melting wax. Candle quartz is said to be a light bringer for the planet and those who have incarnated to help the earth change vibration. It also carries the properties of quartz, highlighting the sole purpose and focusing on the life path, it assists in putting ancient knowledge into practice. Candle quartz is said to create tranquility and confidence. It is also helpful in understanding how the physical body is damaged by emotional and or mental stress, and for healing the heart.*

Lucy was listening to A'nas' description of her second crystal and again she felt awed and honored. The qualities of these two crystals were so beautifully amazing that Lucy had tears starting to swell up in her eyes. She couldn't help it. She felt the love and greatness of their properties and it had touched her heart in a big way.

A'na had taken notice to Lucy's reaction and knew that Lucy was actually "remembering" working with crystals from a past life. They were accessing a spot in her heart that was ready to be activated. It gave A'na a wonderful feeling to be witness to seeing this reaction. She did not say anything to Lucy but just observed and kept it to herself.

"Lucy, would you hand me the third crystal, please?" asked A'na. Again, Lucy reached into her backpack and found the third crystal. It was larger than the other three and she had to be careful not to drop it. A'na took the crystal in her hand and looked at it for a few seconds. This crystal is called Fenster Quartz. It has natural triangle formations within the planes of the crystal. These planes can be traversed as an inner landscape and stimulate clairvoyance. In addition to carrying the genetic properties of Quartz, Fenster Quartz heals dysfunctional patterns and outgrown emotions and is excellent for sending healing light and for energy work that requires a high vibration. It can throw light on the past-life causes of addiction and remove them. It too is a high vibration stone.*

Lucy just sat shaking her head as tears continued to swell in her eyes. She had no idea of just how special the crystals that her grandfather had given her were so very special. She somehow knew that they were meant for her to use.

Ok, let's take a look at your fourth crystal. Lucy reached into her backpack and retrieved that last crystal. Your fourth stone is called Black Tourmaline. This stone protects not only the earth but also protects against electromagnetic disturbance, radiation, and negative energy of all kinds. It not only carries the genetic properties of Tourmaline, but it is also the most effective blocker of psychic attack and ill-wishing. It instills a positive attitude no matter what the circumstance and stimulates altruism and practical creativity.*

A'na glanced at Lucy for a moment as she was describing the qualities of her fourth stone and she too knew that they were meant for Lucy's use. She also knew that it was Lucy that had placed the stones on this land long, long ago in another life. She again kept this information to herself for another time, perhaps.

It seems that Lucy was given four very special stones that had been earmarked for her use many thousands of years ago.

A'na was not surprised by this combination. Each has very profound and specific properties for working in the light of our Source. A'na was curious how Lucy's grandfather had come by them to give to her. "Lucy, will you tell me the story of how your grandfather came by such crystals?" asked A'na "Sure, Lucy said. It is kind of funny. He knew that I like crystals. He told me he had found them in the garden and said nothing else. Again, I asked grandfather to tell me about finding the crystals and he replied that he had found them in the garden. Then one day he started talking about having the springs cleaned out with an excavator. He said the soil that was removed from the springs was then brought up to the garden and plowed in. That is how he had found the crystals in the garden. A'na had a grin on her face knowing that the crystals had made their way into Lucy's hands in such a profound way, just as they were meant to. She loved seeing Spirit in action. All of the attention to detail that is required and everyone playing their part in creating a miracle! The Angels always have their hands full! The Universe always conspires to inspire.

Lucy and A'na gave each other a big hug before calling it a day, as it was getting late, and Lucy needed to get back home. "Lucy, be sure to bring your crystals tomorrow and we will meet at the creek and go to my ship together and begin the process of healing the large quartz crystals. "Can you meet me a little early, say 9 am?" asked A'na. I am going to need your energy and vibration to help initiate this process if you are willing to do so. Lucy did not hesitate with her response of "YES." Although she was sad about A'na departing someday she would not hesitate to help her heal the quartz crystals that would allow her to make the trek back to her home planet, Mentaka. Lucy had so many thoughts going through her mind as she made her way back home. She had many questions she wanted to ask A'na.

A'na knew there are no coincidences, only Spirit at work making things happen that need to be in our lives. That evening, as she did her sunset meditation it was her intent to allow the memories in that she needed to know at this time. Lucy and the phenacite crystal were no coincidence! There was so much more to know about this situation.

As A'na prepared for her sunset meditation she too, had many thoughts going through her mind, many questions she wanted to ask but knew she needed to be patient as all would be revealed as needed. She prepared her blanket in the meadow by the ship. She again grounded herself to Mother Earth and sat upon her blanket cross legged. She took in several deep cleansing breaths. As she allowed herself to just breathe and relax, she found herself yet again, on Mentaka. This time she was at the "Cave of Rebirth." She was there for her sister Raina's remains. She and Raina were twins. They loved each other dearly and although A'na understood each soul has its own path to travel, it was still sad to let her sister go. Raina had told A'na that she had received the urgings of spirit to take this next journey, as that is what she was being called to do. She needed to be a solid foundation of light elsewhere. It was a call that had gone out across the universe and Raina was responding to that call. She had felt it deep in her soul.

Raina and A'na had many discussions about the "Cave of Rebirth" and her choice to leave her family and her planet. She wanted to be in service for the ONE and she felt that it was right with her soul. A'na and her family completely understood and supported Raina in her decision to leave for her next journey. Raina had received a higher calling. Each knew in their hearts that they would see her again. Yes, there would be sadness at the thought of missing their sweet, beautiful Raina. She had brought her family much joy and they were happy for and proud of her decision to assist the universe in a most beautiful way. She had always had a big beautiful and open heart.

Raina had spent much time in meditation preparing for her next journey and was excited to see where it would take her. After this decision is made, there is a waiting time of six months before one is allowed to enter the "Cave of Rebirth" for this specific reason after receiving the CALL. There is much work to be done by the individual as well as much meditation. It gives the individual time to reflect and to be sure this is what they really want to do. It also gives the family members time to reflect, to adjust and to make final preparations. As the day drew closer to Raina's transition the family had a large celebration in her honor, as was traditional. All were invited. It was a beautiful celebration of life. There was a lot of music and singing. Raina was presented with a special bouquet of roses to take with her into the cave. The next day she would enter the cave and make her departure.

A'na remembers Raina had chosen a beautiful purple robe to wear into the "Cave of rebirth." It had great spiritual significance to her and represented her deepest love for our Source. She planned to carry the bouquet of roses to be by her side. She, like A'na, had an affinity for the roses. She also chose many beautiful crystals to be carried in a basket with her into the cave as well as candles she would light after she entered the cave and prepared for her ritual. A'na would be the one to take the crystals as a remembrance of her beloved Raina.

The cave entrance would be closed to all others as they knew that Raina would be in deep meditation after she entered the cave. Two sentries were posted to either side of the cave entrance. Others would replace them after a time. Transition in "The Cave of Rebirth" is the most sacred ritual an individual does on her planet. The 72 hours passed slowly for her family, but they would be ready afterwards for her cremation. Not far from the entrance was the altar for cremations. She would be cremated in her royal robe of purple. Her body was carefully and lovingly placed upon the altar on a bed of grasses that would burn quickly. Her ashes would be collected and spread in the waterfall pool and the surrounding rose garden. A beautiful memorial was planned to say farewell to one they love so much, one so easy to love. The whole planet of Mentaka would rejoice with the family.

A'na remembers that she too had gone into meditation as she knew her sister had entered the "Cave of Rebirth" that morning before sunrise. She had done so in support of her sister. A'na knew this would still be difficult for her to accept; not having Raina by her side, laughing, giggling, and just being herself. A'na remembers as she came out of her meditation, she again had tears in her eyes, this time from remembering her sister and their discussion before her transition. Her heart melted as she sat there reflecting on the present situation. It became very clear to her. She would keep it to herself. It was not the time to tell Lucy any of this at the present time. Lucy would have to figure this out on her own, in her own time. It would only make leaving Lucy even more difficult for A'na.

A'na had many thoughts as she prepared for sleep that night. She would be leaving planet earth soon and that meant that she would also be leaving Lucy, one so easy to love. Lucy had become a part of A'nas' world and she Lucy's. There was great love and mutual respect between them. A'na had shared and taught Lucy much about her planet Mentaka and their beliefs. She had given Lucy a bright hope for herself and for her planet's future. Lucy would help to bring it into the fifth dimension! She would be a bright and shining light for many. Lucy would be able to give many the hope that was needed to carry on, to move forward.

Chapter 17

A'na's Departure

The night went by slowly for both A'na and for Lucy. It seems they both were feeling the pains of A'na's departure. They both had put on a happy face for one another, but it was not easy for either to do. They both put on a brave face for the other. It was easier for A'na, she had the experience of a 5th dimensional life and many, many years of living life with a 5th dimensional perspective. She knew there were no accidents. She also knew in her heart that she would see Lucy again. While on the other hand, Lucy was a young girl on the brink of a grand awakening, letting go of the strings, beliefs and perspectives of a 3rd dimensional reality. She was in the middle of two worlds and letting go of A'na would be hard for her to do. Lucy was feeling the despair of imagining being without A'na, of being alone. Lucy was fighting this battle with her emotions while trying to balance the spiritual truths that A'na had shared with her. All she could do was to keep reminding herself about the spiritual truths. She would take in a deep breath while reminding herself of all that A'na had shared. If she did not do this, she felt like she was in quicksand and could not breath. She chose to BELIEVE!

They had met at the creek the next morning as they agreed. Lucy had brought all four of the crystals, not just the phenacite, just in case the other crystals may be needed. A'na told Lucy they would need to ground themselves after they arrived at the spacecraft and then a 30-minute meditation would be needed before working with the crystals while setting their intent on healing the large crystals. A'na also indicated they would need to cleanse Lucy's crystals and set the intent for their usage as well. All in all, it would take over two hours to prepare for the work ahead of them. Lucy nodded and agreed with A'nas instructions. They were both fairly silent as they walked through the woods to the spacecraft, each having thoughts about the other as they made their way closer to the ship. A'na was not surprised by the heaviness she was feeling in her heart about leaving Lucy. It was difficult. She was also hearing and feeling Lucy's thoughts of dread and sadness. When they arrived at the ship Lucy put her backpack onto the grassy meadow as she and A'na prepared to ground themselves with Mother Earth. Before they could continue A'na wanted to say a prayer, a very special prayer of thanks and gratitude, of recognition and love for the ONE. She and Lucy were about to do sacred work and A'na wanted to honor the healing work they would be doing. A'na also wanted to call in the spirit of her healing mentors and ascended masters to assist her in healing the crystals that are used to propel the ship. They would be allowing the energies of those assisting from the other side to flow through them. A'na and Lucy stood facing each other, with eyes closed, as A'na led them in sacred prayer. Next, A'na and Lucy prepared to ground themselves to Mother Earth. A'na verbally asked Lucy to imagine and see it in her mind's eye as she asked Lucy to send her silver connecting cord down into Mother Earth's core and to set the hook, as she herself was also doing. She then asked Lucy to imagine sending her love and light energies down to Mother Earth and to see herself receiving Mother Earth's love and light energies into her body as she imagined and saw herself become an infinity symbol giving and receiving these same energies. A'na then repeated these words as Lucy joined in. "And so it is, and so it is, and so it is, and it is so! And so it is!" They gently opened their eyes, and a smile was upon their faces as they prepared for the thirty-minute meditation. A'na went into the spacecraft to retrieve the blanket for them to sit upon while meditating. Lucy found herself looking into the sky above and wondering about all that had transpired that summer with A'na by her side. Lucy had come so far from where she was when she first met A'na and yet as she looked at herself, she knew she had not changed physically but from the inside, her thoughts and beliefs were completely different. Her world was completely different. She felt like a different person, yet the same. She felt a freedom she could not yet explain.

As A'na came out of the spacecraft Lucy's attention span returned to the task at hand. A'na spread the blanket out neatly on the ground and both sat down, legs crossed and back straight. Their hands were rested upon their laps with the index finger and thumb touching one another. Both took in a few big breaths through their nose and out through the mouth. A'na gave Lucy a few basic instructions for their intent. "Lucy, I want you to see the two large crystals in your mind's eye. See them healed and perfect. Keep this thought in your consciousness. See your phenacite crystal healing them with her energies." asked A'na quietly. Lucy nodded in agreement as she shut her eyes. A'na and Lucy sat in silence for thirty minutes, their minds focused on healing the crystals. After the thirty minutes had passed, they both opened their eyes as they both stood up and stretched. Few words were exchanged between them, although Lucy was full of thoughts, she knew A'na could hear. Lucy bent down so she could reach into her backpack and handed A'na the phenacite crystal. A'na took the crystal and placed it in her palm. She took her left hand and with her right hand, she made several hand gestures encircling the crystal. She then made some more hand gestures and set the intent for the crystal to be used for the highest and best for the One, that is being used in healing another on this day, in this time and she also asked that it always be used for the highest and best good of the soul using it today and into eternity. A'na then told Lucy that she would need to hold her hands in a certain manner while setting the intent that they would help to assist in the healing of the fractured quartz, while A'na held the same intent and also held the phenacite pointing towards the fractured crystal. They sat on the ground facing the big crystals to be healed. They needed to be comfortable as they would be doing this process in thirty-minute increments so as not to get too tired. A'na was not sure how long it would take in this dimension and atmosphere. It may take several days of healing work and intent, or it may take less. She would just have to see what happens. A'na reminded Lucy to keep an open mind and see the quartz crystal already healed in her minds' eye. The day went by fairly quickly as she and Lucy stayed on task healing the two large crystals. After five hours A'na thought it was time to stop for the day and start over tomorrow. She and Lucy would meet at the creek tomorrow morning and walk back to the ship together. It would give them time to talk and have some fun together. A'na walked Lucy back to the creek with the nature creatures by their side. Lucy loved seeing the creatures walking with them. They were so gentle to one another and to her and A'na. Lucy had become quite fond of them. She had always loved all of nature. As they walked, Lucy recalled an incident when she was about six years old. She and the neighbor kids were waiting on the bus when a crow landed on her head. She remembers she was not scared, she thought maybe it needed some of her hair for its' nest. She couldn't wait to tell her mom and dad.

Lucy's dad was always weaving stories about the fairies to Lucy. He had initiated the interest she had in the woods and what she called the "magical' kingdom. Lucy, her mother, and her father all loved being out in nature. Although Lucy did not know it at the time it was a love she would have in her heart throughout her life. It would keep her heart eternally young. She had not shared this story with anyone before. A'na found it very amusing and was grinning at Lucy while shaking her head. It wasn't long before they had arrived by the creek. "I will see you in the morning, Lucy," said A'na while giving Lucy a big hug and kiss on the cheek. "Lucy, I want to thank you for all that you have done, your help, the phenacite crystal. Everything! I love you dear one." and she headed back towards the ship, creatures in tow.

Lucy was very restless and tossed and turned most of the night. She knew it was the thought of A'na leaving and returning to Mentaka. A part of her wanted to go with A'na, but she knew in her heart that she could not just leave her family and Earth. She had so many thoughts going through her mind, but finally, she must have drifted off to sleep and found herself running a bit behind schedule the next morning. She did remember to pack some snacks and water for her and A'na. She had left the backpack and crystals with A'na. She headed towards the creek and found A'na and the nature creatures already there and waiting. All greeted one another and started towards A'na's ship by the edge of the wood. Once there, the same rituals were repeated as yesterday before they began to work with the crystals healing the fractures. A'na and Lucy had completed two healing rounds when they decided to take a break and have some water. It was while sitting there that A'na noticed the one crack was gone like it never was and the fracture was beginning to heal as well. Both A'na and Lucy jumped to their feet and began to giggle and hug one another. Lucy was in awe. She had never seen such a miracle in action. She was amazed, to say the least. "Do we continue, or do we stop?" Lucy asked. "HMMM we may want to give it one more session," replied A'na, and so they did. When they stopped there was complete silence. The crystal's break was as if it had never happened as well. A'na could make her trip back to Mentaka! It was so bitter-sweet. The happiness was followed by the fact that A'na would be leaving Earth very soon. She would return to her home planet where her life was, her family, but she would be leaving Lucy who had become her family as well and this is what was laying heavily on both of their hearts. A'na had to remind herself that there are no accidents. Everything happens for a reason. She had said these words aloud to remind Lucy as well. Lucy had put on her brave face again but the thoughts she was having did not support it. A'na knew she was about to cry and came closer to hug her and let her know that she would be fine. She reminded Lucy she had a mission she needed to complete while in this life. A'na told her and reminded her that they would always be just a thought away from one another. Love is eternal and so are you, Lucy. Never forget that you are an eternal being of light. You are the stuff that stars are made of. Lucy hugged A'na ever so tightly as tears streamed down her face. She looked at A'na as she was shaking her head in agreement and remembering all that A'na had shared with her.

The two sat on the blanket in silence for a while as the woodland creatures came in close. They too understood fully what was going on. Word had spread quickly that the crystals were healed, and they understood A'na would be leaving planet Earth soon. They would miss A'na greatly. As Lucy looked up and into the woods, she saw many more creatures heading towards them. With the crystals healed all knew A'na would be leaving Earth and returning to Mentaka. All wanted to be sure to say their farewells to A'na before she departed home. They came in even closer one by one as A'na put her arms around them or her hands on each one and gave every one of them a warm and loving hug. Even the butterflies were fluttering all about. It was so very touching that Lucy had tears running down her cheeks.

She would never forget this event that was happening before her very eyes. It touched her heart in such a way that she could not explain. It was a beautiful sight of true love and respect for one another.

It was getting late and A'na said, "We better get you back home before it starts to get dark, and your parents get worried." Lucy and A'na stood up and headed towards the creek, everyone together. It wasn't long before they were at the creek. Lucy looked at A'na and wondered when she planned to leave. "Don't worry Dear One, I wouldn't leave without letting you know well in advance. How about we wait till another day has passed? That way we can just do whatever you want tomorrow. How does that sound?" "That sounds great, A'na. What do you want to do?" replied Lucy. For now, we can just agree to meet here at the creek tomorrow morning around 9. Sound good?" asked A'na. Lucy nodded in agreement, and they gave each other a hug goodbye.

A'na turned and headed back towards her spacecraft, creatures by her side. She was in deep thought thinking about all that had transpired since her arrival on Earth. She was excited to return home to see her beautiful planet and her loving family even though she would miss her dear Lucy. She had returned in time to do her sunset meditation. The blanket was already laid out. She sat down and crossed her legs one on top of the other and took in several deep breaths before finding her quiet place. She sat quietly, then before her mind's eye was her sister Raina. She was again at the edge of the wood, wearing her purple robe. A'na was walking towards her, closer and closer. She stopped and received these thoughts, "Trust yourself. It is true. I will see you again. It is time to remember." And then Raina was gone. As A'na's eyes opened she found herself repeating those words over and over. "Trust yourself. It is true. I will see you again. It is time to remember."

The next day she was by the creek as promised to Lucy. Lucy had been there and was waiting on A'na. "Wow, what a pleasant surprise," said A'na. "I know, right?" They sat on a rock by the creek and listened in silence to the sounds of nature, the water gently going over the rocks, the birds flying in and out of the woods, the bird song, the wind moving the leaves. It was beautiful and relaxing to just sit and listen. "A'na, how did we heal the crystals?" asked Lucy. "Actually, Lucy we did not heal the crystals. What we did was to allow the healing energies to come through us. We were acting as a conduit so that the healing energies could pass through us to the crystals. These are the loving healing energies from the other side of the veil. I can tell you more if you like. I can give you what is called an attunement. This will allow you to awaken more fully to the energies that are available to you for this purpose. An attunement will provide a direct connection between you and the universe. Let me explain it a little more fully for you. Attunements work by clearing energetic pathways in the body causing a positive shift in consciousness which creates a harmonious energetic connection with the universe. "Did that answer your question, Dear One?" asked A'na. Is this something you would like to know more about?" inquired A'na. "We can do this today before you leave for Mentaka?" asked Lucy. "Yes, I can get you started and give you the attunement. You will have to research and find others who can get you the experience learning and using your knowledge and gifts." A'na responded. "Let's do it!" Lucy said in agreement. "OK, then let's do it!" replied A'na.

A'na asked Lucy to stand as she made several hand gestures over Lucy's head, she then asked Lucy if she could sit on a big rock and close her eyes and place her hands on her lap, palms up. A'na then took Lucy's open palms and blew over them while holding her breath with her tongue in the top of her mouth as she held her breath. She stepped behind Lucy and did something with the crown of her head. Lucy didn't know what she did, but she felt something. A'na then asked Lucy to open her eyes. Lucy did not know what to expect. She opened her eyes and felt no different and stated as much to A'na. "Dear one, what were you expecting? Remember this is subtle work and it will do and be as it is supposed to. Just allow. Just allow. Be patient with yourself and be gentle with yourself. You have experienced much since I have been here with you. Remember just because you do not see, hear, smell or feel something does not mean that it is not real, or not present. There are many, many energetic levels of life going on before your eyes that you are not yet aware of. Remember there are many, many dimensions. And there is much change coming! Much change. When you are ready, the energy will be there, ready and waiting." A'na answered.

A'na told Lucy when you do any sacred healing work you want to always, ground yourself with Mother Earth. Before each healing session or work you want to always ask our Source and your sacred assistants that it be done for the Soul's highest and best. In other words, you want to put your human ego to the side and allow the Universe to do its work. What the Soul may need and our ego may think we need can be very different things.

Lucy, you can and will be a great healer if that is what you want, but you must always remember that healing does not come from you but through you. Remember you are a conduit. You can benefit from this healing energy coming through you. That is a nice plus. Remember to go over the chakra information we discussed a while back.

You will have your client sit or lie down upon a massage table on their back to begin with. Let them know they will be fully clothed. Have them feel relaxed before beginning. The only thing they have to do is to allow the energy to do its work. When working on clearing the chakras, you will start at the crown chakra and work your way down the ladder as you have your client lie on their back and on their stomach if you wish to address more emotional issues. You can incorporate the colors as needed with the use of crystals and even colored fabric laid upon each chakra. You can also learn about using essential oils in your healing practices. You will learn to trust your "gut" instinct as you do this work with others. And as you do this work, you will get more comfortable with doing it. It will become second nature to you. You can lay your hands upon the chakras and as needed just above the chakras. You will begin to sense when there is a decrease in the energy centers and when there are blockages. After you have finished working with each chakra, cleanse the energy field like wiping off a chalkboard or turning on what you call windshield wipers. This removes the energy that you have just released. I enjoy using feathers to clear the energy that has been released. Lucy, you can use this healing energy with your plant and animal friends too.

The discussion of when A'na was going to leave had not yet been addresses, but it was time to do so. A'na gave Lucy a look that told her it was that time. "Lucy, I thought I would leave in the morning hours so that you could be there and see me off if you want to. How do you, want to proceed? Do you want to be there as I leave or would you rather I leave without you being there?" she asked Lucy. "A'na, I want to be there when you leave. I want to see your spacecraft lift off the ground and go up into the sky beyond my sight. I want to be a part of this grand time in the history of the planet when you leave in your spacecraft and no one knows but me and our friends, the woodland creatures are aware of it. It is our secret for now. I want to see this so that I never, ever, forget it." she said. And then, she began to cry, big huge tears were running down her cheeks. A'na looked at Lucy and told her it was OK if she cried. She understood. She wanted to assure Lucy that they would never be apart. She would always be in her heart and just a thought away until they meet again on the other side of the veil. "Lucy, you must always remember that love is eternal, just as you are an eternal being of light. This is just one of the lives that you are aware of at this time. Remember this is part of the illusion of a third-dimensional life. When you are ready you will be able to see your life and look upon it as an observer. Remember your mission, Lucy." A'na explained. Lucy was taking in all of the words A'na had just said to her with great intent and as she thought upon them it gave her a better feeling and a better perspective on what was about to happen. She reminded herself what a beautiful miracle A'na had been to her and for her. She was grateful to God, our Source.

The two planned to meet at the creek around 9 am and walk back to A'na's spacecraft together for A'na's departure and take off. They took their time walking, talking, and giggling about their times together. They reflected on their first meeting at Lucy's alternate birthday party and how Lucy had taken A'na by the hand and was introducing her to everyone, only they could not see her or hear her! They both gave a big guttural laugh. Only they knew the real truth.

It had been a fast spring into summer and now A'na was about to take off from planet Earth and return to Mentaka. The Universe always conspires to inspire. This time it involved the 'accidental" landing of what we call an extraterrestrial, into the life of a young girl. Lucy was beside herself as A'na and she gave each other a big long hug. A'na kissed Lucy on the forehead and looked her in the eyes, telling her 'til I see you again, my Dear One, 'til I see you again." She turned and looked at all of the woodland creatures who had befriended her from the beginning and blew them all a kiss as she telepathically told them she would miss them so, how much she loved them, as she told them "I will see you again." They were all very still as A'na made her way into her spacecraft, tears running down A'na cheeks. Lucy and the nature creatures all watched intently, waiting to see if the repaired crystals would allow A'na's spacecraft to lift off. Ana settled into her captains' chair after checking all instruments. She initiated her flight pattern for Mentaka. All systems were a go as she gave a final farewell, waving goodbye to all, before lifting off and out of sight. Lucy and the woodland creatures watched as A'na departed. Her spacecraft was so fast it was as if it had disappeared in an instant before their eyes and she was gone.

Lucy turned and looked at the woodland creatures as she too had tears streaming down her cheeks. She had to make herself move and go back toward her house. She looked at the woodland creatures who had promised to walk Lucy back safely to the creek. You could not tell who was sadder, Lucy or the creatures. A'na had left such an impression with all of them. Lucy thought "it would take some getting used to," as Lucy's grandfather had said after he was feeling the sadness of losing his wife, Anne, Lucy's grandmother. Lucy felt sad and forlorn as she and the creatures made their way to the creek. The walk seemed longer than normal and seemed to take forever. She was glad for the woodland creatures' company and knew she would see them again on a regular basis. Once back home she had gone to her room to reflect on what had just happened and it seemed that as happy as she had been for the past several months she was now the saddest she had ever been in her life. She wailed aloud. She felt that she had just lost the most important person she had ever known. It felt like a part of her own body was missing. She had felt like this when her grandmother had passed. She felt lost. Over the next several days she had mostly remained in her room only going outside to take care of the farm critters and Iris and the rest of the herd. Iris was aware that A'na had departed and how it was affecting Lucy, but she could not do anything to help Lucy with her despair, other than be present for her.

Lucy's parents had also noticed how sad Lucy had seemed over the past several days and were concerned. They asked Lucy if there was anything wrong or if they could do something to make her feel better. She assured them she was OK, but it was so obvious she was not OK. She was not herself at all. She had never felt so low, so depressed. It was not in her nature to let things bring her down to this point and yet there she was. She was not sure how to climb out of the hole that she was in. She slept in most of the days. She ate little and talked even less. Lucy remained in this state for over a week and then one day she woke up and realized that she was in mourning, like someone she loved had passed. She remembered A'na words, "Be gentle with yourself" and so she understood she must give herself time to grieve and heal. It was this understanding that allowed her to do just that, to heal. It seemed that each day she began to feel a little better, going out to the horses and talking to Iris, spending time in the out of doors. It was several more days after, but she eventually ventured to the creek. She sat on the big rock she and A'na used to sit upon. Big huge tears came running down her cheeks again and she whaled out loud for the sadness she was feeling without A'na by her side. When she opened her eyes there were some of the woodland creatures by her side, offering her comfort while feeling their own sadness over A'na's departure. Just as quickly a flock of birds flew in flittering in and out of the trees as she remembered what A'na had said, she is there in the birds that fly, and the creatures that you see. It was as if a light had just been turned on in Lucy's mind. Lucy realized she was just feeling sorry for herself for too long. A'na is fine. Lucy told herself she had a mission to fulfill. She had promised A'na she would do this. Slowly but surely she pulled herself out of the quicksand she had been in and began to find herself out of her slump. She began to study about crystals, the chakras, and all of the other things that A'na had shared with her. The crystals that her grandfather had given her were now much more to her than pretty stones to admire. She worked with the crystals, cleaned and cleared them and set her intent with each crystal having a specific purpose. But most importantly, she began meditating each day. She would go to the creek or to an area in the out of doors where she felt comfortable and would not be interrupted. She found herself controlling the thoughts she allowed into her head and her life was yet again turned around. She began keeping a journal. Each day she would write something down about her thoughts or feelings or the impressions she would get from her meditations.

Chapter 18

A'na's Return Trip to Mentaka

A'na knew it would be very difficult for Lucy to let her go. Lucy was a young girl in this life on the cusp of a full awakening from her third-dimensional slumber while A'na had a lifetime of knowing and understanding what being in a physical vessel can present. She was not worried about Lucy because she knew in her heart that she was well on her way to being the observer of her own life. Her trip to Earth was still a bittersweet journey. She had many thoughts going through her mind about Lucy, about their times together and the time she had spent on planet Earth. It was only a few months and yet it felt like a day and sometimes it felt like a lifetime. On the other hand, she was excited to get back to Mentaka and go to the waterfall pool and meditate so she could get more understanding about the whole "accidental" landing. She could not wait to see and hug all of her family and friends, both two-legged and four-legged.

A'na had sent an intergalactic message to Mentaka letting them know she was in space and on her way to Mentaka. She should be there within a short while. Her trip had gone smoothly as she viewed Lucy's beautiful Earth from space. Her understanding of Earth and a third-dimensional planet had been altered a bit.

She had experienced firsthand how the perspectives of a 3D life can be changed overnight allowing one to awaken and know that there is so much more to life than what is before one's eyes. She saw firsthand how the thoughts on a 3rd dimensional planet play into the everyday lives and surroundings of its' inhabitants. She saw what these thoughts and their actions were doing to the population, the planet and to all of her inhabitants, all life on the planet. It was like life was being taken for granted! It was something that A'na could not imagine, especially after seeing it firsthand. A'na knew that life is a very beautiful and special gift that is given to us by the ONE and yet she was given the gift of understanding it even more by landing on planet Earth at this very special time in history.

Lucy was and had been one so easy to love and easy to share her spiritual insights from a fifth-dimensional perspective. She knew that Lucy was to play a key role in the change that was coming to planet Earth. Lucy would be able to offer much comfort, healing, and unconditional love to others as they worked through what is and was ahead of them.

A'na was lost in her thoughts when Mentaka appeared on her horizon as she looked toward her home planet. She soon saw the pink halo that surrounds the planet. Pink is the color of love, and this planet is much like Venus, a planet of unconditional love. She saw all the colors of the watery planet, all the blues, and aquas' from the oceans. She felt her heart quicken as she got nearer. She had never left the planet for such a long time before and was excited to be back home. As her spacecraft was about to land, she saw her family and friends had come to greet her. She saw some of the planets' woodland creatures sitting alongside the landing area. As A'na gently landed her spacecraft and prepared for her departure, thoughts of Lucy trickled through her mind still. She gracefully exited the spacecraft and quickly hugged her mother and father, her other family members, and greeted all the woodland creatures. She gave each a big hug, even the lions, the tigers and the bears! She had a big smile on her face and could not wait to tell everyone about her adventures with a young girl named Lucy on planet Earth. It would be much easier "talking" telepathically. As she would be able to articulate what she wanted to convey without forming words and moving her mouth, although she had enjoyed talking aloud with Lucy. It did not take long and the whole history of how and what had happened had been shared with the entire planet of Mentaka, it seemed. It was very apparent how much this young girl had meant to A'na and the love that they shared for one another. A'na also shared with her family her most recent meditation revelations that she had been having about Raina, the words that she had left with her, "Trust yourself. It is true. I will see you again. It is time to remember." and how Raina seemed to disappear as she got closer to her. She told her family how excited she was to go into the waterfall pool for a very deep relaxing meditation in the water. She felt she had been missing a part of what she had been seeing in her mind's eye about Raina and the words she had left with her. It was now the time to know and understand what she had been missing, not seeing.

She spent several hours just settling in and being with her family and friends a while before doing her sunset meditation and calling it a day. It had been a long journey and she was feeling a bit tired, something she really did not do often. She did not get tired. She thought maybe it was the excitement of being home and the nagging from her gut about the message she had received from Raina. It would have to wait until the morning. A'na prepared her blanket on the ground for a beautiful sleep under the stars and the two beautiful moons above her. She took in a big breath of air, letting it out slowly, and then she was asleep. She awakened well before sunrise making her way to the rose gardens and the waterfall pool for her sunrise meditation. She took her time walking as she knew she needed to be calm and relaxed for this meditation in order to receive, know and understand what information was being given to her by Raina. She knew Raina would make sure she understood the words she was giving to her. As A'na reached the rose garden she smiled and nodded to the roses, sending them a big hello and a greeting of love and friendship as she walked by. She let them know she would attend to them as she finished her meditation. All of the roses understood, nodding in return. They too were excited to see A'na.

As A'na walked to the waterfall pool's edge she gently removed all of her clothing before entering the water's edge. She dipped one foot into the water and then slowly walked into the water up to her neck as she turned on her back floating on the water's surface. The sun was just beginning to rise, and the colors pink, orange and purple were reflected onto the water's surface making it all the more beautiful and welcoming. A'na took a big breath as she also took in and appreciated her beautiful surroundings before letting it out, only to take in another. On the last in-breath, she had found herself in the same beautiful garden where she had been with Raina. She walked closer to Raina and as she came closer it was as if Raina had turned into Lucy and suddenly, she knew, what she had known all along, but was not seeing. Lucy was/is Raina! Raina is Lucy in this life.

She was suddenly awakened and tears were running down her cheeks as she allowed this truth to go through her whole body. It all made sense and she was taken aback by the fact that she had gotten to spend time with her beloved sister in such a special way. She was directly involved with her awakening as the young girl Lucy. They had gotten to share their life together in another timeline, in another dimension. A'na was both honored and elated by her crystal-clear revelation and yet somehow she knew that somewhere in her being she had known the truth of the matter all along. A'na was in awe of such a beautiful and special reunion she had gotten to have with her sister, Raina. It was such a special miracle for her and for Raina, (Lucy). A'na had been brought up to know and believe in reincarnation and yet this event that she had been a part of was so very special to her. The big beautiful tears of gratitude continued to roll down her cheeks as she sat in quiet reflection. She could not wait to share this information with her family. But first, she must attend to the roses as she promised. She dressed herself slowly and started toward the roses, as she approached, the roses were already aware of her thoughts and were enjoying sharing in her joy! They too, knew of the special consequences that A'na had been a part of.

A'na greeted each rose and hummed her way along as she trimmed any dead blooms and leaves from each rose bush. All the while she was thinking about her time on planet Earth with Lucy by her side almost each day. The love they had shared with one another, as well as the laughs and adventures. She was still in awe. The Universe always conspire to inspire. A'na was definitely inspired and awed. She was almost numb with her excitement and realized that had she known the whole truth while with Lucy that it would not be the miracle she saw looking back at the situation. She was part of a very special and beautiful miracle. She got to love her sister in yet another way. She got to love her as another being, not knowing that she was her sister in another life! Love is eternal and that bond is never broken. It goes beyond time, beyond dimensions! The tears continued to swell in her eyes and run down her cheeks as she looked back at the whole situation with joy in her heart. The gratitude she felt was overwhelming. She took her time with the roses as this was a good way to allow all of the beautiful information of this miracle to settle into her mind. She floated along as she worked with the roses and as they cheered her on in quiet celebration.

A'na wanted to shout it from the mountain top and let everyone know what had taken place with her sister Raina as she knew that all would want to know and celebrate with her. She finished up with the roses and said a good bye for today as she headed towards her home to let the others know the conclusion of her meditation with Raina. As she got closer to her crystal home her feelings of happiness had already reached them and they reached out their arms to hug A'na in a warm embrace. She telepathically told them every detail of her meditation and how as she reached to hug Raina she had turned into Lucy. She told them how it all became so crystal clear as tears still ran down her face. She felt humbled by being in the grace of such a beautiful miracle! Her life would never be the same.

Chapter 19

Full Circle

Several years had passed and Lucy was now a young lady of twenty. Although A'na had been gone from Earth all these many years, her memory stays with Lucy every second. Lucy had learned much from A'na and has remembered all of the spiritual truths as presented by A'na. There was one thing, however, that A'na had not told Lucy, for she was in denial herself. It was something Lucy would have to figure out on her own. Lucy felt it in her being and knew there was a secret of some kind. There was a piece of the puzzle that she had not figured out, she had not found. A secret that she wanted to know. Although she missed A'na so much, she knew that A'na was always with her and in her spiritual heart. She knew that they would be together for each other in some kind of way throughout eternity.

She had promised A'na that she would not forget any of her teachings. She also promised she would meditate each and every day for the rest of her life on Earth. As she meditated each day, she would fine-tune the spiritual truths that were hers and hers alone. Lucy had already shared many of the teachings A'na had shared with her to friends and family. She had turned

A'na's teachings into a profession for helping others. It wasn't something she had planned, but it just happened, with her intent to help others.

Lucy had helped many, many people through some very difficult times of chaos and change. Many had lost an entire family; others were frightened to come out of their homes without a mask, even after many years. Fear was still in control. Many had turned into recluses without realizing it. With Lucy's help and others like her, hope was being restored and a new way of being was taking place. It was happening one by one. The time was now.

It was through her meditation that she had discovered something that she had felt in her heart for a long while. She realized that she had gone to the "Cave of Rebirth." She saw it in her mind's eye. She saw herself in the sacred robes that are worn as one enters into ritual at the mouth of the cave. She saw herself and she looked much like A'na! She felt what this action brought to her soul. She had tears of joy running down her cheeks. She said to herself, "I am Raina!"

As Raina, she also felt the bittersweet goodbye she had given her family. She remembers hugging her sister, A'na, as tears ran down her cheeks. She remembered the goodbye hug and the feeling that was so familiar. It was A'na! A'na was her twin sister on Mentaka. This realization jolted her out of her meditation. She was shaken to the core but wanted to know more. "I lived on Mentaka!" she said aloud. As Raina, she had made the decision and had chosen to journey on. She had gone to the "Cave of Rebirth." This must be why A'na was so very important to her and why her spacecraft had "accidentally" landed on Earth.

Her mind began to race as she began to understand so much more than she thought she could. She would have to wait until her next meditation to know more; for now, her brain was a flurry of questions and thoughts. Her curiosity was piqued. She must trust her spiritual heart and her gut and not the ponderings of her egoic mind. She told herself to settle down. The answers would come when she was ready.

She had learned much from A'na, and she was sure that A'na had remembered and knew too. A'na had been sent by the Universe to jolt Lucy from her slumber, to remember her mission, to remember it all, to know in her spiritual heart what has truly happened. As A'na had already taught Lucy all she had to do was to hold the "LIGHT" that she was, to anchor that light to the earth as it was so needed at this time.

Lucy knew that A'na would not have interfered with her remembering the "Cave of Rebirth." A'na would know this was something Lucy had to do on her own. She was almost trembling with all of the memories coming into her being. She was humbled by it all and at the same time elated. LOVE IS ETERNAL! Her consciousness knew the whole story, but it had to make its way to her mind at its own pace. If she had any doubts about any of her teachings, they were now gone. A fire had been started, and Lucy had much work that she wanted to accomplish. She knew just how to begin to "see" and connect with A'na again. The crystals were going to assist her to communicate through time and dimensions. This was a new chapter in Lucy's life. She felt she had a purpose, a very special purpose.

Lucy always knew she had been a part of a very special miracle when A'na had come into her life from another planet and shared her spiritual teachings with her from a fifth-dimensional perspective. If she had any kind of doubts what soever, they had now been dissipated. She now knew that she had been part of an even greater miracle, to have been with her sister from another life, to love her and enjoy her company while in another human vessel. Lucy felt so very humbled and grateful as the tears came flooding out and she was overtaken with a joy filled heart in gratitude to the ONE! She was the onion. She understood exactly what A'na was talking about when she referred to peeling the onion. Yet here she was being the onion. It seems that as life comes at us every day we "forget" the softness, the preciousness of it and we develop layer after layer until we cover that very soft spot in the middle. It is that vulnerableness that speaks to our very core as an eternal being of light! Life is precious. It is special. It is a gift! Life is a GIFT!

If she had learned nothing, she had learned that there are no accidents! A'na's spacecraft had landed here on Earth, in North Carolina, so that she could reconnect with Lucy in this timeline, on planet Earth during a time of great change. Lucy was beginning to "remember" her past life on Mentaka. The memories had begun years ago with the gentle nudging she was getting when A'na first appeared in the woods.

Now on her twenty-first birthday, the memories seemed to be flooding back into her consciousness. Each day as she meditated, she would receive a "new" memory from her past life on Mentaka. Lucy called them snapshots. Every time she would close her eyes in quiet reflections, she would see the snapshot of a scene, the beautiful memories of life on Mentaka.

Lucy was elated! As she sat in silence by the same creek she and A'na had visited so many times, out of nowhere, she could see Mentaka in her mind's eye. She was there by the "Cave of Rebirth." She could hear the waterfall as it made its descent onto the ground below. She could smell the freshness of the water in the air, and she could hear nature all around her. She felt very calm and very peaceful. She awakened from her meditation with a feeling she could not describe. It was more like she was remembering the feeling of being there in her body. It was a memory of her loving sister and her family on Mentaka. It was a memory she was enjoying as she sat with a smile on her face.

Back to Mentaka

A'na knew without any doubt that Lucy had discovered the truth of what she had known for a while, that they were sisters on Mentaka.

All of the memories kept coming to A'na about her sister, Raina, and all the fun, the sacred work they had done together, and her sister's decision to go to the "Cave of Rebirth." It was a decision that had not come easily for Raina, but she knew it was in the best interest of her soul's journey that she takes the next step in her journey of the soul. She could do much good, and she knew somehow, some way that she would receive the assistance that she needed to get the job done.

A'na also knew that she and Lucy would always be in each other's hearts and never apart. Love is eternal. She decided to meditate with the intent of communicating with Lucy. She felt that Lucy was probably in an open space in her heart where she could receive her communication. Several years had passed and she was sure that Lucy was continuing in her meditation and sacred work and would be able to communicate with her as well. A'na had deliberately waited to contact Lucy, waiting for the realization of her past life as Raina had coalesced into her being. A'na knew this would empower Lucy as she trusted the truth of the reality of her life as Raina, her sister.

The story of A'na, of Raina and Lucy are not one that seems to happen every day, but what if that is what happens, and we are just not realizing it? We come and go in and out of each other's lives, playing our parts and forgetting to see what is beyond our eyes. A'na and Lucy were able to put the pieces of the puzzle together and to "see" beyond what their eyes could not see. They had to trust their spiritual hearts and allow. The universe always conspires to inspire. The unconditional love of these two sisters is what kept their hearts open. They believed in something greater than themselves. I ask you to do just that: BELIEVE! We are the stuff that stars are made of! YOU are the stuff that stars are made of. We are eternal beings of light! We are an extension of our Source.

With much love, A'na and Lucy, 'til we meet again!

Bibliography

Bibliography for A'na's Gift

D"Ambrogio, Dr. Kerry, The D'Ambrogio Institute 2021

Hall, Judy, The Encyclopedia of Crystals (Fair Winds Press, Beverly, MA., 2006)

Phillips, Marcia A., Seven Portals to Your Soul (Bridges of Unity Loves Park, Illinois, 2004)